Also by Ellis Sharp

Novels

The Dump
Unbelievable Things
Walthamstow Central
Intolerable Tongues
To Wetumpka
Lamees Najim
Neglected Writer
What Vronsky Did Next
Twenty-Twenty
Alice in Venice
Full English

Short Fiction

The Aleppo Button
Lenin's Trousers
(with Mac Daly) *Engels on Video*
Driving My Baby Back Home
Aria Fritta
Quin Again, and other stories
Dead Iraqis: Selected Short Stories

Non-Fiction

Sharply Critical

For everyone who went over the fence ...

Ellis Sharp

TO WANSTONIA

Zoilus Press

First published in Great Britain by Zoilus Press, 1996

Reprinted 2021

ISBN 9780952202844

Cover photo of a decorated tree on Claremont Road, London, by the author.

Contents

"I need a drink," Rachel managed to say.

"Take heart," I said. "The beginning of the change has set in."

Philip K. Dick, Radio Free Albemuth

Spiders

To flinch, once, meant to cut up or to flay. It was a verb born from the mouths of expatriate Danes and Norwegians, cold solitary saltwater-splashed figures with knives clenched in their hands and blood on their sleeves and boots. They stood on desolate beaches beneath misty rainswept promontories by Whitby, Lochinver, South Ronaldsay, hacking up seals. *Flense; flinsa; flunsa:* flench, flense, flinch. Ghosts, now; a livelihood of entrapment, dissection and flaying wiped out by industrial whaling, cheap chemicals and factory products.

To flinch, nowadays, means to draw back or to recoil or to wince. It carries a sense of avoidance, of springing back and swinging back; to flinch can mean, at a stretch, to revert, to reverberate, *to have repercussions*. Nowadays the verb "to flinch" is unlikely to bring to mind those cuddly, whiskery, dewy-eyed icons of the environmentally concerned. It is spiders, not seals, that provoke flinching, and cause people to screech, and to knock over their little plastic Body Shop bottles, and to run out of the bathroom in a red panic.

Spiders have a poor image, thanks to the baleful influence of shifty, upwardly mobile entertainers like William Shaxberd, and that ubiquitous brat Miss Patience Muffet. Fortunately the Austen-Curbins have never shared the popular antipathy towards spiders. If I find a spider trapped in the vast, bleak Saharan wilderness of an enamel bath I have no qualms at all about encouraging it on to the palm of my hand and then tossing it out of the window. On hot summer days, clad only in swimming trunks, lying on my back on a lawn, I have permitted spiders to wander my kneecaps, jog across my stomach and even to stretch their webs from my ear to my shoulder, without feeling any need to scramble blindly to my feet and flap about wildly with my *Portable Nietzsche*.

Spiders have always had a special place in the affections of the Austen-Curbins, for had it not been for a distinguished ancestor's interest in the species none of us would ever have existed. I refer to the fruitful and pleasurable attachment which George Austen formed with a fifteen-year-old girl whom he encountered in a dry ditch in Hampshire in late June 1782. George was observing with interest a couple of plump *Steatoda bipunctata* preparing to mate. Some people exchange significant glances whilst taking tea at the Pump Room, Bath; some people make mutant suggestions amid a disco's throb; the male *Steatoda bipunctata* wanders around the web of his female friend in a seductive, erratic manner, waving his large palpal organs.

On this particular June afternoon, in the ditch in question, the female showed distinct signs of interest, and began making a series of shameless, unambiguous plucking motions, before retiring in the conventional way to her tubular retreat. George watched, fascinated, as in a frenzy of anticipation and excitement the male ran to and fro, spinning a mating bridge. Next it entered the retreat and enticed out the female with a pretty display of leg vibrations. Aroused, the female scuttled eagerly on to the mating bridge. She hung there in a debauched posture, oblivious to the presence of my ancestor, who watched, entranced, as the male lunged lustfully with one of his palps until at last he succeeded in inserting it. Penetration was maintained for eighty-seven minutes, during which time a plump, lascivious girl named Mary came strolling along the ditch, tapping George on the shoulder and making him jump. With the aid of grimaces and hand-signs George drew her attention to the biological drama being acted out before their very eyes. Hand in hand they watched as the male withdrew his palp and hunched alongside the female, a little depressed perhaps, perhaps mentally sketching immense suspension bridges and five-barred gates and latticed nameless things. The spider chewed thoughtfully upon his palps for some considerable time before at last returning to the object of his desire with renewed stridulatory movements of the abdomen. Urgently he thrust in another of those trembling palps, at which Mary, shining-eyed, could bear it no longer. With beads of sweat upon her upper lip and a pungent coastal whiff about her waist, she tore at George's loose summer breeches and pulled him down.

One of the Austen bastards in due course consorted with a Curbin and our branch of the family was soon solidly established. Should you wish to investigate matters further I am confident that you will find that our blood link with Jane Austen is every bit as authentic as the Knatchbulls or the Austen-Leighs. Indeed, it has long been a minor source of interest and amusement in our family. There is nothing an Austen-Curbin enjoys more than glancing at the Austen family tree in a Jane Austen biography and chuckling over the erroneous blank that invariably appears beneath the entry *George Austen (1766-1827).*

Like the Austen-Curbins, George himself has long been marginalised into near invisibility by those pap 'n' prettiness purveyors known as the Austen industry. He rates, at best, a sentence or two. George is the idiot of the family; the genetic freak; the hideous embarrassment. With grotesque inaccuracy he is usually referred to, if at all, as mentally defective. In fact he was simply a spritely epileptic who also happened to be deaf. Either was enough to doom his chances in that narrow, oppressive land known as Regency England, and Jane Austen's dull, conventional parents hurriedly ejected him from the family home and dumped him with low, obscure, forgettable relatives in a suitably distant parish.

George's subsequent life as a pirate is a tale with rather more interest and plausibility than that concoction of adolescent fantasies known as *Treasure Island,* but would involve me in divagation – a literary trait which, above all others, I detest. Consequently I shall shun the malformed twigs and twiglets of that gross, puffy, blistered, scum-encrusted Austen family tree, with its bundles of diseased libertines, corrupt, grasping royalists, petty-bourgeois toadies, its foul Governor of South Carolina, its slippery, glistening Master of Balliol College, and its purple-cheeked triple-chinned 8th Baron Chandos. Likewise I shall have nothing whatever to say concerning the

Austen-Curbins, or my great-grandfather's friendship with Lenin, or my father's extraordinary adventures amongst the tribesmen of Nambuangongo, or my dead sister and her role in the mysterious incident which occurred in a nondescript Lowestoft hotel on that same, hot, sticky afternoon when Ambassador MacPherson was assassinated in Tunis. My intention is simply to correct certain misconceptions which are commonly held about George's famous sister, and her much-read scribblings.

The opportunity to do so arose unexpectedly when my cousin Jack was crushed to death by a car on 6 October 1988. He was standing on the pavement on Heath Road, SE8, examining a curled leaf in a bramble bush. Observing a gash in the leaf. he prised it open and found, as he had rather been expecting to, the brittle, emaciated body of a dead female *Steatoda bipunctata*. Beside the corpse an earwig was feasting on the blue silk-swathed eggs. Evidently deep in thought, Jack seemed not to hear the Ford Sierra as it spun out of control. The vehicle mounted the footway at 74 mph and crunched Jack against an adjacent brick wall with tremendous force, killing him instantly. I subsequently inherited Jack's semi-detached in Penge, in the attic of which, while hunting for a nice plump *Theridion tepidariorum,* I stumbled upon the moth-eaten carpet bag containing an old and very dirty manuscript entitled *Finis* as well as a battered notebook with many missing pages, the recent dual loss of which in a fire should not, if probability and the probity of an Austen-Curbin still count for anything in modern society, permit even the faintest traces of doubt regarding the integrity and authenticity of what follows.

The manuscript, some five-hundred loose sheets of brittle foolscap, made no sense at all. Written in ink in a tiny, spidery longhand, it seemed to have been composed according to some simple yet bafflingly incomprehensible code. *Them uniting of means the been had, Derbyshire into her*, it began, and went on for page after page in a similarly opaque manner. Many of the pages were splashed with repellent brown stains, as if the entire manuscript had been compiled by a deranged soul with a shaky wrist and a fondness for oxtail soup. The notebook made more sense, but was full of scrappy entries about someone called Pierre. It contained meaningless lists, random statistics, unfinished sketch-maps of unidentifiable places. Irritated beyond endurance, I tossed the manuscript and the notebook back into that crumbling, dusty carpetbag.

They remained there for a year, forgotten in a cupboard. If an intriguing specimen of *Ciniflo fenestralis* had not scuttled there one bright crisp morning they might be there still. Remembering in a dark flash my spectral cousin and his dark dull funeral, I remembered also his enticing attic, alive with short squat bodies, bundles of green eggs and a specimen with a swollen palpal bulb. Dragging out the carpet bag, I extracted *Ciniflo fenestralis,* dealt with it in the usual way, then hauled out the manuscript.

It was when I reached the very last sentence that I finally understood. *Wife a of want in be must fortune good a of possession in man single a that, acknowledged universally truth a is it.* Of course! What an idiot I was not to spot it earlier! *Finis* was *Pride and Prejudice* written backwards! Only a little extra research was required to establish that the handwriting was indeed that of George Austen's sister. *Finis* was nothing else than the long-lost manuscript of George Austen's sister's first novel! For reasons known only to herself – whimsy? an iron self-discipline? an avant-garde impatience with the dreary conventions of linearity? – George Austen's sister had composed the narrative in reverse order.

The circumstances in which she had written her story puzzled me. The notebook was clearly in George Austen's sister's handwriting, and appeared to be contemporaneous with the manuscript. There was even what looked like the figures 1797 scrawled on one page, as if indicating the year in which the entries had been made. But who was Pierre? There is no one named Pierre in any of the biographies of George Austen's sister.

I made another intriguing discovery. George Austen's sister's whereabouts between September 1796 and April 1798 are distinctly elusive. The whole of the year 1797 is an utter blank. This is confirmed both by her biographers and by her correspondence. Examine, if you have the stomach for it, any edition of George Austen's sister's *Collected Letters*. Note that on Sunday 18th September 1796 Jane Austen wrote one of her characteristically gossipy letters to her sister Cassandra ("What dreadful hot weather we have! – It keeps one in a continual state of Inelegance"). Note that the next available letter is dated Sunday 8th April 1798 and is a brief note of insincere condolence on the death of William Hampson Walter, her father's half-brother.

Numbed by Jane's chatter about balls and dancing and agreeable young men and Miss Biggs and Caroline's spinning-wheel and the heat and a visit from Lady Hales and the venison from Godmersham and Miss Fletcher's purple muslin and Mary Harrison's gown, it is easy enough to drift into a stupor and entirely overlook that vast, gaping hole into which innumerable words have slid forever – expunged, burnt, obliterated in one way or another. All the letters Jane Austen wrote over that period of eighteen months between September 1796 and April 1798 have been destroyed.

The conventional explanation is that Cassandra's fiancé, Thomas Craven Fowle, died in February 1797, and that Jane's letters at this time would have contained much that in later years would have revived painful memories for her sister. Cassandra, quite naturally, tore up these letters. Another explanation is that Jane Austen simply didn't write any letters at this time, being too busy comforting her sister. Such vacuous speculations are, of course, the work of men and women who utterly lack both the family knowledge of an Austen-Curbin, and access to the manuscript of *Pride and Prejudice,* let alone a notebook of tantalising jottings. The role of Thomas Craven Fowle as the ostensible cause of those missing letters interested me. My interest quickened when I discovered that Thomas Craven Fowle is almost as margin-alised in the J. A. story as her brother George. Where did Fowle die? The West Indies. What did he die of? Yellow fever.

What was he doing there? He was with a British military expedition. What was the expedition doing?

Silence.

You can't expect Jane Austen scholars to concern themselves with obscure military ventures in remote foreign regions, can you? Of course not. Be reasonable.

Thomas Craven Fowle died on an island called San Domingo. It was the most profitable slavery colony in the world, exporting raw sugar, white sugar, indigo, cotton, hides, molasses, cocoa, tobacco and rum. In August 1791 there were mass uprisings by the slaves against the French plantation owners. In 1792 the French Government sent 6,000 troops to put down the slave revolt. The slaves defeated them. In a panic the plantation owners invited the British Government to protect them. Lt. Col. John Chalmers wrote a memorandum to Pitt: "The advantages of San Domingo to Great Britain are innumerable and would give her a monopoly of sugar, indigo, cotton , and coffee."

September 9th, 1793, 900 British troops land on San Domingo – an advance party, to be followed by the greatest expeditionary force ever to leave the British Isles. By the end of 1796, after three years of war, 40,000 British troops had died and another 40,000 were permanently unfitted for service as a result of injury or sickness. Thomas Craven Fowle was with the expedition, although in what capacity isn't clear. He died of yellow fever, unaware that precisely ten years later the poet William Wordsworth would publish a tribute to Toussaint L'Ouverture, leader of the slave army.

A plump, crushed specimen flattened among the pages of *Finis* provided a luminous clue. The third and fourth legs were smeared across the second paragraph of p. 235; the rest, intact, albeit with a vicious crack across its sugared-almond-sized abdomen and with intermittent damage across the cephalo-thorax, obscured half-a-dozen words on the opposite page. The corpse, unmistakeably, was that of a *Heteropoda venatoria*.

What was a large, squashed, long-dead tropical spider doing amid the manuscript of *Pride and Prejudice?* The answer is starkly obvious. George Austen's sister wrote her novel in the West Indies. On the island of San Domingo, to be precise. Thomas Craven Fowle was clearly the original reason for her presence on the island (J. A. probably substituting at the last moment for her sister Cassandra, who was unexpectedly indisposed). The exact circumstances in which she abandoned the society of the plantation owners and joined the army of rebellious slaves will never be known. Certain entries in the notebook lead me to believe that she established a relationship with a slave named Pierre, gave birth to a stillborn child in August or September 1797, and stayed to mourn Pierre's death in battle on September 30th. By November she was probably back in England. Here her suntan began to fade, and with *Finis* completed she worked quietly at revising the manuscript which eventually became *Sense and Sensibility*. Note, in this regard, the otherwise curious description of Marianne as "brown".

My theory explains a great deal about the manuscript of *Pride and Prejudice*. The pungent smell of smoke and the pages blackened at the edges testified to the difficult circumstances of composition. The brown stains were obviously blood. The enigmatic smears in Chapter Fifty-One were powder, spilled from a musket. Other blotches and inky specks spoke mutely of San Domingo's rich, humming insect life. Mysterious sketches and doodlings in the margins suddenly made sense as maps of Fort Dauphin, Bois Pin and Marmelade.

Lurid tropical images surged and cascaded in my mind. Jane Austen, flat among the ferns, her arms around Pierre's black, shining, muscular body. Jane, Pierre and the other slaves, rolling a massive rock down a hillside, aimed at the column of redcoats filing along the valley below. Jane, Pierre and the others digging trenches in the road and covering them with branches, and the horsemen plummeting down on to the rows of sharpened spikes. Jane, Pierre and the others blazing away at the redcoats from the shelter of the trees, then melting away among the dense undergrowth. And all the while, with a pistol in one hand and a pen in the other, with a bloody bandage draped over her arm and a swarm of mosquitoes humming about her temple, George Austen's sister sweats and scratches herself and scribbles furiously – *Neighbourhood the through speed proportionate with and, house the through spread quickly news good the* – her cool, faraway tale of chaises and parcels and bandboxes.

There is no evidence that Jane Austen ever spoke of her tumultuous experiences in San Domingo in 1797. Her silence is strongly reminiscent of Arthur Ransome's. If nothing was known of Ransome's life prior to 1925, would anyone have ever believed that this gentle, walrus-faced old buffer with a string of children's books to his name, whose main interest in life was pottering about in boats, had once been a passionate supporter of the Bolsheviks, a friend of Lenin's, and a scathing critic of the whingeing, hand-wringing Liberal's favourite Trojan Horse, the Constituent Assembly of December 1917?

The shadow of San Domingo is inescapable in Jane Austen's later life and writings. Admirers have sometimes been troubled by what appears to be a gratuitous streak of nastiness in her letters. In October 1798 she made her notoriously callous observation that "Mrs Hall, of Sherborne, was brought to bed yesterday of a dead child, some weeks before she expected, owing to a fright. I suppose she happened unawares to look at her husband."

Tasteless? Malicious? Heartless? Perhaps – but behind that brittle screen of cynical wit we can surely glimpse the tormented remembrance of the time she squatted naked behind a coffee bush and squeezed out a bloody, lifeless half-caste infant. The memory of Pierre, and of her dead child, and of those tens of thousands of fallen black slaves, weighed on her later years like a nightmare. When, in 1808, Jane Austen made enquiries about the appearance of the dead body of her sister-in-law Elizabeth this was not the morbid, prurient curiosity of a ghoulish spinster, but rather the detached scientific interest of a woman well acquainted with mass graves, tropical putrefaction, maggots, discoloration and the truly astonishing speed with which rigor mortis solidifies a soft, fresh corpse.

The name of San Domingo can nowhere be found in Jane Austen's writing. Her response to the death of Toussaint L'Ouverture on April 7th, 1803 – her reaction to the Declaration of Independence by the Republic of Haiti – is nowhere recorded. This was entirely deliberate. It was not until *Mansfield Park* and *Persuasion* that she even felt able explicitly to broach the topic of slavery. In all her writing after 1797 there are nevertheless innumerable moving, unmistakeable allusions to the immense impact which the San Domingo slave rebellion made upon Jane Austen. In Lyme Regis, on Friday September 14th, 1804, she wrote to Cassandra: *Your account of Weymouth contains nothing which strikes me so forcibly as there being no ice in the town.* Coded allusions to the West Indies are rarely quite so explicit as this.

The following year we find Jane writing to her sister from Goodnestone Farm:

We had a very agreeable evening, and here I am before breakfast writing to you, having got up between six and seven; Lady Brydge's room must be good for early rising.

Three o'clock. – Harriet is just come from Marianne, and thinks her upon the whole better. The sickness has not returned, and a headache is at present her chief complaint, which Henry attributes to the sickness.

Was there ever a more caustic portrait of the inanities and egotism of the English ruling class? The scorchingly satirical portrait of Marianne's headache is a brilliant touch, and forms an explosive contrast with the ensuing blank space that stretches to the foot of the page. It is a space that speaks eloquently and suggestively of white colonialist oppression and of that painful void in the writer's biography – a void of blackness, a dead child, a dead lover, a plain of ashes, obscured by the white, obliterating clouds from fields of burning sugar cane. But if Jane Austen's *Letters* form a crucial record of one woman's vigorous, revolutionary critique of bourgeois society, how much more powerful are the novels!

Pride and Prejudice was not published until 1813. Some time during those long years of obscurity Jane Austen chose to reverse the order of her narrative and return to linearity. Bearing in mind the publishing conventions of nineteenth-century England it is impossible to blame her. Even in its more conventional form this novel testifies to the author's vigour and wit in creating an ostensibly innocuous, faraway fictional landscape amid the flies and stench and rotting bodies of San Domingo. It reminds me of J. G. Farrell, conjuring up *Troubles,* his masterpiece of 1920s rural Irish life, amid the hubbub and screechings of New York City in the 1960s. But by the time she'd returned to Hampshire, Jane Austen's need to construct an imaginary England was gone. Surrounded by hedges and fences and pallid hillocks she was able to pour out her bottled-up agony in the vicious satire of *Sense and Sensibility.* When Edward tells Marianne of his preference for neat, ordered, flourishing landscapes – *I have more pleasure in a snug farm -house than a watch-tower – and a troop of tidy, happy villagers please me better than the finest banditi in the world* – we note how razor-sharp the irony, how unmistakeably Jane Austen measures her fatuous bourgeois character against the bloody realities of San Domingo – and finds him lamentably wanting.

Tracing the influence of the San Domingo rebellion on the Austen *oeuvre* is not something that can be accomplished overnight. I do not pretend to offer anything more here than a modest, pioneering, preliminary sketch. I shall leave others, with better eyesight, more stamina and superior qualifications, to write the innumerable articles, theses and books which will be required. Biographers of George Austen's sister will, of course, have to start again from scratch; for many academics, and even for many ordinary readers, the necessary readjust-ments will not be easy. From some quarters, no doubt, a vigorous defence of the old, traditional ideas will be mounted. There may even be shrill, neurotic cries of "hoax!" No matter. Let them say what they want to. I shall not flinch.

B is for Baby and Bolshevik

With admirable independence the fiery old fellow ... had illustrated to his goggling history class how the Bolshevists, far from being the child murderers in the *Daily Mail,* followed a way of life only less splendid than that current throughout his own community of Pangbourne Garden City.

Malcolm Lowry, *Under the Volcano* (1947)

1

The end, did someone say? Fool! The end? Far from it. Quorne came back. His cheeks were the colour of oatmeal. He considered "Blinch" (a brisk yet intriguing name) and "Firgang" (the name of the household on M. Dmitrovka Street in Moscow where Chekhov stayed in 1891, at a time when Vladimir Ulyanov was busy writing polemics against the Narodniks, including *On the So-called Market Question* (1893), which shows an impressive grasp of the second volume of Marx's *Capital*) but in the end adopted the pseudonym "Inkpin", after the leader of the internationalist wing of the British Socialist Party, formed in 1911.

His tan? You have assumed, as I did, that Inkpin worked on the sphinx by day. Inkpin fooled us all. He laboured under the pale glow of moon and stars, pausing only to glance up admiringly at Horologium, "The Pendulum Clock", one of the constellations representing mechanical instruments intro-duced in the 1750s by Lacaille and which, as with so many of Lacaille's maddening constellations, is faint and obscure.

Inkpin was averse to all forms of artificial illumination. It had something to do with the religious training he had received as a child. His upbringing still sometimes poisoned his reasoning. At three in the morning he put the finishing touches to the great nose, was instantly tormented by doubts which are available for inspection in the first published draft of this story, and reduced it in seconds to a blazing puddle crackling smokily in the dirty sand.

Inkpin turned and ran.

Escaping via the Gold Coast and travelling only on Tuesdays, Inkpin arrived back at Stony Stratford and looked in the mirror. It was probably September. His hair was receding above both temples, leaving a spear-shaped wedge of blackness which gave him an astonishing resemblance to Telly Savalas in *Cape Fear* (1962). He had lost weight and bore a strange scar on his left shin but after a cup of Earl Grey (one sugar) he felt better. He rented a shabby room in a war-damaged house near Gildersleets, from where, probably in March, he set out on foot to the converted medieval manor house by the river, to attend an interview for the post of tutor to Walter Augarde.

"Cool your heels in here!"

Inkpin heard the door close behind him. The butler had evaporated. Removing his shoes and socks, Inkpin glanced urgently around for a suitable source of refrigeration. There was nothing, nothing at all.

The door opened.

"What are you doing?" the butler asked, in a grey voice.

Inkpin had adopted a crouching posture, his knees pointing towards Yokohama and his bottom swaying an inch or so above a square of stained ochre canvas.

"I should have thought that was obvious," he retorted, irritably.

Walter was the six-year-old son of Harvey and Emerald Augarde. It was Emerald who conducted the interview, while Walter sat in the corner, cutting the legs off toy soldiers with a Swiss army penknife. Each of the six candidates were asked six simple questions. Only Inkpin was able to answer all six.

The questions.

1. What is the main task of the historical period through which all the advanced countries (and not only the advanced countries) are now passing?

2. What was the commonest colour of the extra-terrestrial spaceships which penetrated our atmosphere in 1973?

3. What was "Rotted as by a charm" in the first version of Wordsworth's *Prelude?*

4. Can a negation ever be final?

5. When Lenin posed the question "What is to be done?", what was his answer'?

6. Who said that a toddler only becomes a child "when he [*sic*] ceases to be a wayward, confusing, unpredictable and often bolshy person-in-the-making and becomes a comparatively cooperative, eager-and-easy-to-please real human being"?

2

Inkpin looked sombre. Trembling slightly, he said, "Investigate, study, seek, divine, grasp that which is peculiarly national, specifically national in the *concrete manner* in which each country approaches the fulfilment of the *single* international task, in which it approaches the victory over opportunism and 'left' doctrinairism within the working-class movement, the overthrow of the bourgeoisie, and the establishment of a soviet republic and a proletarian dictatorship – such is the main task of the historical period through which all the advanced countries (and not only I the advanced countries) are now passing!"

Emerald Augarde nodded and smiled.

"Red," Inkpin continued, adding: "There may well be a connection with the red rain which fell across France on October 16th and 17th, 1846. It is said that this rain was so vividly red and so blood-like that many French people were terrified. As for that miserable apostate and bourgeois lackey, Wordsworth, he was referring to his own life. The relevant lines, I believe, go something like this:

Rotted as by a charm, my life became
A floating island, an amphibious thing,
Unsound, of spongy texture, yet withal
Not wanting a fair face of water-weeds
And pleasant flowers.

Needless to say the slippery oaf toned this down in the wheedling 1850 version. The image is a striking one (had Wordsworth been at the drugs cupboard again?) and inevitably brings to mind the floating island of Loch Ness, mentioned in Richard Franck's *Northern Memoirs* (1694), an author attacked for rendering himself 'obscure, and sometimes altogether unintelligible, by his affected pedantry and obscurity', a baseless criticism, his description of the floating island – 'a natural plantation of segs and bullrushes, matted and knit so closely together by natural industry' – perfectly lucid, and in no way justifying the conclusion of the monsters-in-Loch-Ness-mob that Franck was alluding to an extinct marine dinosaur."

Inkpin paused in order to thrust the handle of an ultramarine toothbrush up his left nostril, and then, upending it, down his throat, hurriedly clearing away some troublesome mucus. In spite of its weaknesses, he had always been fond of Malcolm Lowry's first novel.

"You ask if a negation can ever be final. Absolutely not! Every negation is negated by the spread of opposites which spring up in its wake, interpenetrating, rubbing against each other, causing sparks and glowings. As Engels said, consider a single grain of barley. If it falls on suitable soil and gains access to heat and moisture it germinates and hence the *grain* is negated by the *plant*. And what happens next? Why, dear Madame Augarde, the plant flowers, is fertilized, ripens and dies. In short, we witness *the negation of the negation*, with the original grain of barley multiplied twenty- or thirty-fold. A man or woman who has grasped this fundamental point is well placed to begin the manufacture of whisky. When the grain begins to sprout, place enormous quantities on screens over peat fires, add gallons of brown burn water from an obscure highland region, ferment the ensuing mash with yeast, distil the alcohol twice and mature in old casks. Wait (according to taste) five or ten or fifteen years, and then consume. Goes well with bloater sandwiches."

After a mild – so mild as to demand that "mild" be erased

and replaced by "gentle" – heart-attack, Inkpin was able to answer the last two questions.

"If my memory is correct Lenin wrote *we may meet the question, What is to be done? with the brief reply: Put an End to the Third Period.* He was writing in 1902, of course, and was referring to the first three periods of Russian revolutionary socialism, alluding specifically to the period of disunity, dissolution and vacillation which began in 1898."

Mme Augarde nodded in an animated way.

Inkpin smoothed his fading hair, moved on to the terminal teaser. He glanced at the second hand on his water-resistant Lorus quartz watch, purchased two days earlier to replace the one he had lost in Hackney on the fourth day of the No M11 Link Road campaign's "Operation Roadblock", when attempting to trespass on the Temple Mills Bridge site of the link road, where an overbridge was being built by civil engineering contractors Christiani & Nielsen, a firm founded in Copenhagen in the year Lenin climbed a mountain close to the Castle of Chillon in the company of Maria Moïsseyevna, who used the pseudonym "Zver", and who remembered how, reaching the summit , with beneath them stretching acres of blinding snow, dark belts of pines, verdant valleys and lush Alpine pastures chequered with glorious greens, she was about to declaim appropriate passages from Shakespeare, Byron, when she was cut short by Lenin, who, seated and silent, suddenly shouted, "All the same, those Mensheviks – they're all wrong!"

The second hand skipped merrily on its monotonous circular way, prodding Inkpin towards death, its interminable silent jerks making him think of muddled Liberals and deluded members of the Labour Party, going round in circles as they halted then lurched, halted then lurched after improvements for everybody in a capitalist society run for the benefit of a corrupt and ruthless ruling class. The thought was so grey, so uninspiring, that his mind at once launched itself with a tremendous velocity through time and space, landing by great good fortune on a copy of *Le Comte de Gabalis* by the Abbé de Montfaucon, a volume which set out the Rosicrucian Doctrine of Spirits, describing how the four elements of the earth are inhabited by sylphs, gnomes, nymphs and salamanders and which Alexander Pope made great use of when writing a second and enlarged version of his "Heroi-Comical" poem *The Rape of the Lock* – which, curiously enough, sent the eighteenth line of Canto I shooting into Inkpin's consciousness ("And the press'd Watch return'd a silver Sound"), a topical allusion to the new, fashionable "Repeater" watches, which sounded the hour and the quarters, and which brought him back to all that is clockwise and mortal.

He remembered, how, later that day, he had succeeded in climbing the security fence by the Green Man roundabout and had, with others, occupied a green crane, holding up work on Contract 2B of the M11 Link Road, the Advance Sewer Contract. He remembered, too, how he always cheered up at the sight of a twenty-four hour digital clock registering seventeen minutes past seven in the evening.

"Leach," he said hurriedly. "A risible formulation, incidentally. Her paradigmatic child is obviously geared to the requirements of late capitalist society."

"How late?" interjected Mme Augarde.

"Three or four minutes to midnight."

Inkpin scratched his scar. "What chiefly surprises me is that in a baby manual first published in 1977 (and no doubt still in print today, on this charming afternoon in June) we should encounter the adjective "bolshy", signifying *uncooperative* or *bloody-minded* or *difficult,* when as anyone who has read their Reed or their Serge or their Ransome knows full well that *co-operation* was the essence of Bolshevism (for as the quotation on the entrance to the Assembly Hall, Forest Road, Walthamstow, from the writings of that proto-Bolshevik William Morris has it, FELLOWSHIP IS LIFE AND THE LACK OF FELLOWSHIP IS DEATH), the Bolsheviks co-operating with, and winning the approbation of, the mass of workers – even, in fact, of the peasantry, in an astonishing and still inspirational way."

"Point of view," squeaked Walter, who had read his Wayne

Booth, waving his scarlet penknife. "That's what it's all down to. *Bolshy* is an adjective drenched in capitalism. Non-co-operation forsooth! What a fucking joke! Non-co-operation with the structures of the capitalist state, that's what Bolshevism was all about. Non-co-operation with the rabble of compromisers, opportunists, vacillators and Czarists who made up the bourgeois democratic Provisional Government of February 1917! Or, in a wider sense, non-co-operation with other capitalist forms, such as the authoritarian family structure, the father or mother snapping at Dick to devour all his sugar-sodden Shreddies otherwise he won't get a contaminated burger for his tea."

"I could hardly have put it better myself," beamed Inkpin, unaware that in the version of "B is for Baby and Bolshevik" published in *Massacre* 2 (1991) Walter had been silent and this speech had in fact belonged to him. A moment later, however, the story resumed its original form.

"Am I correct, Walter, in thinking that you are re-enacting in the corner two of the all-too-frequently forgotten events of that historic year 1917?"

3

Little Walter looked up with a smile, three crumbs and a smear of orange and tangerine marmalade prepared with 43g of fruit per 100g upon his face. He laid down a handful of mutilated, limbless soldiers and said: "Correct! In the first instance I was re-enacting the meeting of war invalids held in a Moscow amphitheatre in March. On that occasion a crippled infantryman began to hurl abuse at the crippled officers who had attended the meeting. *Not long ago you swine were beating your men with knouts and fists! Now you dare to stand in the way of the masses!* There was a roar of protest. Footless foot soldiers banged their sticks and crutches in approval. Limbless officers trembled with fury and waggled their stumps. Suddenly a one-legged Colonel lashed out with his crutch and whacked a one-eyed Lance Corporal. An armless cook kicked a blind Captain,

24

who swung his walking stick, breaking the nose of a disfigured rifleman. In no time at all the great imperialist war was being re-enacted in every section of the amphitheatre. Shell-shocked, wounded, mutilated soldier blundered against shell-shocked, wounded, mutilated soldier, exchanging blows, cursing. Crutches were hurled in a parody of high-explosive shells. Blind men's sticks were lunged into the stomachs of the enemy like blunted bayonets. Ah, if only Artaud could have been there! And so the answer to your question, Herr Inkpin, is YES – although my humble attempt to represent that grotesque episode with my plastic infantrymen crudely painted in Third Reich colours must seem itself a re-enactment of such self-evident superficiality and playfulness (not to say ABSURDITY) that I think the only appropriate term for my little perform-ance would be *post-modernist*."

Here Mme Augarde coughed delicately and said, "His vocabulary is coming along, don't you think, Monsieur Inkpin? Walter, tell Signor Inkpin the words you learned yesterday."

Walter scowled. "Oh, very well, mother. Incatenate. Glucic. Sudarium. Myxon. Nixon. Spiegelschrift. Properispomenon. Prosopography. Prosopopoeia. Ichthyodorulite. Thropple. Tap-cinder."

"Nixon?" interjected Inkpin, baffled.

"A confirmed liar. A dishonest personage. A crook. A dissembler. A mountebank. A saltimbanco. A war criminal. A devious right-wing opportunist. A cozener. A vindictive fraud. A thimblerigger. A shyster. A slyboots. A friend of the Clintons. A distinguished American statesman whose long career must be judged in its entirety. *Q.v.*: Dicky, Tricky, Cambodia, Genocide, Slippy, Slippery, Devious, Dog, Dollars, Finance Capital, Launder, Siphon, Imperialism, Capitalism, Barbarism."

Inkpin, who knew it paid to increase your word-power, hastily scribbled in a little notebook.

Mme Augarde frowned. "You missed out ideopraxist."

"Please, mother," retorted Walter, a little crossly. "I have not yet finished what I was saying. I was about to tell Comrade Inkpin that the second performance by my hopelessly disfigured toy soldiers was of quite a different episode. The scene shifts to the icy and snowbound city of Petrograd. The time: six weeks later. To be precise, April 17th. The event: the demonstration of the war invalids. And what happened? An immense number of wounded servicemen limped or hopped or wheeled or dragged themselves from the hospitals of Petrograd and advanced upon the residence of the Provisional Government. There, legless, armless, blind, swathed in bandages, they chanted the slogan WAR TO THE END. They were the losers, the defeated. The demo had been organised by the bourgeois liberal Kadet Party with the aim of squashing the Bolshevik demand for an end to the great imperialist war. After all, if you have lost a leg in a war you do not want to be told that your leg was lost for a cause that was worthless, do you? But the demonstration was ineffective. You see, the numbers of soldiers with two eyes, two legs, two arms, ten fingers and thumbs and a conventional collection of 206 bones nicely functioning alongside gristle, flesh and veins vastly exceeded those who hadn't. Everyone with two eyes in their head and a complete set of bones was a lot less keen on WAR TO THE END than the Generals, the journalists, the politicians or the bourgeois intelligentsia. Let's face it, even having a finger or a toe amputated is no joke, requiring as it does an incision down to the bone at the level of the base of the phalanx uniting the two extremities of the palmar flap, followed by retraction of the soft tissue, the opening of the joint, the cutting through of the lateral ligaments and the flexor tendon, ending with the joining together of the two bloody flaps with a few fine sutures and a neat gauze dressing. Horrible!"

Mme Augarde felt obliged to interrupt. "Walter, darling. I do not think Field Commander Inkpin has quite finished what he was saying."

4

"I was simply- complexly! – going to remark on the fact that Ms Leach seems wholly unaware of Lenin's own deep fascination with babies, disobedience and child-rearing," whispered Inkpin, in a Dublin accent.

At this point in his life (before the unfortunate episode of the shears and the drunken midget) Inkpin was almost six feet tall, spare, with large bones, including a magnificent femur and a strikingly impressive clavicle. Had he been wearing a black vizard mask you might have deduced, from the lower part of his face, that he was a man of strong character, with a thick, hanging lip, and a long straight chin, suggestive of resolution pushed to the length of obstinacy. Without the mask his countenance expressed profound earnestness rather than high intelligence (but looks are often misleading). His eyes were piercing and he was often able to assist cobblers robbed of their tools or small malicious children with balloons to burst. His forehead indicated causality and comparison, with deficient ideality, inducing strict logicality from insufficient premises. He walked with a slouching gait and with an air of abstraction. His dress was very plain, his stockings tight, his necktie preposterously loud. He had many Magliabechian habits. He was fond of narrating a harrowing and desperate story about a passage down the Straits of Macassar and had once or twice been mistaken on Paddington Station for Wilhelm Gottsreich Sigismond von Ormstein, Grand Duke of Cassel-Falstein. He seemed to be in the best of health. He was dead within the year. "I don't quite –"

5

"I refer to the booklet which Lenin finished on 27th April 1920, in which he addressed the question of tactics in the international working-class movement, including such posers as 'Should revolutionaries work in reactionary trade unions?' In it Lenin rounded on Sylvia Pankhurst for arguing that British revolutionaries should have no dealings with the Labour Party but instead pursue 'the direct road to the communist revolution'. The whereabouts of this road are a fascinating question. Is it to be found at a junction with the

Great North Road – now better known as the A1 and A1(M) – leading, at last, to Victoria Street, London SW1? Decades later the matter remains unclear. Lenin's belief that British revolutionaries should participate in the activities of the Labour Party on the grounds that British workers would then soon become disappointed with their leaders and swing towards communism was obviously over-optimistic. What I find interesting in all this is that in chastising so-called "'left-wing" communists', the great Bolshevik leader described their political position as *an infantile disorder*. This brings us to the heart of the matter – the all-important question of Lenin, infants and medicine."

"But first," said Mme Augarde brightly, "tea and biscuits."

The butler came in, sweating and red in the face, his shoes and socks sodden with blood. What sort, he wanted to know, proffering a large circular green tin along the sides of which were displayed, in strictly contrapuntal order, scenes from everyday Viking life and moments from the historic siege of Lyme Regis. "Wheatmeal digestive for me, please," cried Walter. Inkpin chose a chocolate finger. "And I'll have a Wagon Wheel," said Mme Augarde.

As they sipped their tea they chatted about duodenal ulcers and duodecimo editions and defunct self-styled socialist states. For ten minutes or so they discussed the continuous bleeding from the anus which is the consequence of a large and active duodenal ulcer. Walter I proudly displayed his biology home-work – a crayon drawing of three dark, glistening stools of the sort called *meloena*. Then Mme Augarde asked Inkpin if he had ever visited the Union of Soviet Socialist Republics. Inkpin said no.

"More's the pity. I understand it was a place where there was considerable interest in Dinsdale's Hump. There are any number of paperbacks. Even the new regime is taking an interest. You may have read about the recent promising lines of enquiry. You perhaps have not yet seen the latest authoritative scientific report by the Dinsdale's Hump Centre for Binocular Research. It unambiguously concludes:

1. Cannot Be Reconciled with the Laws of Physics.
2. Folie à Deux.
3. "It all begins, as I've told you, with a man called Brown."
4. Amazement.
5. "Egg-shaped."
6. Alien Origin.
7. All delight doth itself soons't devour.
8. "All the events of that night have a great importance."
9. A curiously shaped barrel spiral galaxy in Camelopardalis, beyond the range of amateur telescopes.
10. Caused considerable annoyance.
11. Eleven, at least.
12. A Highly Intelligent Vegetable Not Handicapped by Emotion or Sex.
13. "This thing must not be swept under the rug."
14. Often on a Tuesday, at dawn.
15. Uneasiness and agitation.
16. Edgar Allan Poe.
17. Disbelief.
18. Strawberry flavour.
19. Unrelenting Marxism.
20. "Appears to interact with radar and generate Kodak photographs."
21. Amnesia.
22. Baku.
23. "Kaspar! Makan!"
24. Ambleside.
25. Anomalous Acceleration.
26. Yesterday.
27. Everything, as you see, depends on the way things are put.
28. *Nominus mollire licet mala.* ·
29. Appears as an "immense collection of commodities".
30. Too late to dream of flying, of limpid fountains, smooth waters, white vestments, and fruitful green trees.
31. "With a harpoon, can you believe!"
32. Mattock. Wrenching Iron.

33. Should Be Investigated by Properly Trained Technical Personnel.

"Hmm," hmmed Inkpin. "It's possible, I suppose. But to revert, as everything in the end must do, to Lenin, infants and medicine."

"Lenin, did you say?" gasped the butler, who at that moment was brushing crumbs from the carpet. "If I might be so bold ..." A bulge under his top hat yielded a hidden copy of *The Vile Life and Miserable Death of the Fanatic Lenin* by Rupert Barker-Porker. "As the blurb makes plain, this is an objective and scholarly biography which shows beyond any doubt that the infamous Russian was a brute right from the very moment that he kicked the midwife in the midriff, lashed out at the doctor and dribbled over his poor, tired mother. Lenin was a man in the grip of dark impulses of destruction. The index says everything:

LENIN (Ulyanov, Vladimir llyich):
nihilism of, 29
torments neighbour's budgerigar, 5
fights Plekhanov, 61
ignorant of the 1603 star map of the German celestial cartographer Johann Bayer, 144
prefers Germans to English, 56
trousers, 4, 13, 78, 83-9, 123, 202, 564
lust for power, 3, 7, 78, 99, 103, 122-78, 403
kicks blind one-legged priest, 87
attacks Cadets, 197
enjoys films of Luis Buñuel, 205
known as William Frey, 302
observes Walthamstow through telescope, 156
duels Martov again, 208
craving for celery, 308
attached to lnessa Armand, 235
repressed homosexual tendencies, 3, 12, 303, 578
rages against Mensheviks, 203, 234, 256

butter, 580
takes ferryboat to Sweden, 400
duodenal ulcer, 566
writes articles for cycling magazine, 301
writes letter about frogs, 235
holiday in Aleppo, 388
writes letter urging insurrection, 379, 382
criticisms of *Reds,* 455
arranges assassination of Tsar and family, 466-68
cruel smile, 2, 7, 14, 34, 122, 340, 450, 560
absorbed with power, 471, 488
interest in transvestism, 278, 297
escapes from bandits, 504, 534
storms out of This is Your Life, 587
warns against capitalists, 538
visits Lyme Regis, 408
spits at nun, 17
Proclamation Against Budgerigars, 467
writes savage letter to Kursky, 550, 557
enjoys Nirvana album, 409
warns of split in Central Committee, 564
refuses to mow sister's lawn, 230
enjoys Jack London story, 599

Barker-Porker slightly mistranslates the title of the monograph you were referring to earlier, when I was crouched at the door, my ear pressed against the keyhole. He calls it *The Infantile Malady of Communism.*"

"Hmm," hmmed Inkpin. He seemed about to speak but the butler beat him to it.

"Barker-Porker establishes the following facts about Lenin's early years:

"1. Lenin's mother's maiden name was Blank. It is therefore not surprising that he became a nihilist.

"2. Lenin was born on April 22, 1870. He was a typical cusp Taurean – stubborn, wilful, over-excitable.

"3. Lenin's behaviour while being born was disgraceful. He

screamed, assaulted medical personnel, urinated on the bed and was sick over his mother.

"4. Lenin's older brother Alexander was quiet and reserved, good-looking, with no malice in him. He walked, even as a toddler, with a princely stride. Lenin, on the other hand, was an unruly, noisy child given to tantrums. Also he slouched.

"5. Lenin learned to walk long after normal children do. He was always falling down and bursting into tears. Years later the couple in the house next door admitted that their enjoyment of the double album *Janis Joplin in Concert* had been "significantly marred" by the noise Lenin had made as a child.

"6. One fall, when Lenin was three or four, was quite bad. He may have sustained brain damage. This would certainly explain how he came to develop the bestial doctrine of Bolshevism.

"7. Lenin's sister Anna remembered how he was always breaking his toys. He farted and picked his nose. Anna, on the other hand, never farted or picked her nose. She was a sweet-tempered, kind little girl who gave cups of tea to old ladies and put out saucers of milk for orphaned hedgehogs. Lenin was so maddened by this that he broke the legs off her three toy horses. Also he broke her ruler.

"8. In every family there is usually someone who plagues everyone else, has tantrums and wild rages, and becomes bald and moody in later life. Sometimes such individuals dedicate their entire lives to mischief-making and killing royalty. It is not known if Lenin had bad breath but it seems very likely.

"You see!" cried the butler. "Lenin wanted a world without servants! Without butlers of any kind! He would have put people like me out of existence! He was as wicked as a post-modernist author! Just let someone like Lenin take two or three taps at a keyboard and people like me may find themselves whisked through time and cyberspace, waking up in an armpit, or St Petersburg the morning after or never waking up at all! Lenin was the sort of person who would have pressed F6 without compunction, coating me in white, then pressing *Delete*. Hideous. Is it any wonder that children refuse to obey their parents or smash up property as long as copies of *The Infantile Malady of Communism* are left in the world?"

("Idiot!" thought Maisie, wandering in from another story. "No one can possibly hope to understand *'Left Wing' Communism: An Infantile Disorder* who does not understand the context of the months in which it was written, i.e. April and May 1920, when there was a massive growth of support for bourgeois centrist parties, the consequence of the radicalis-ation of very large numbers of European workers. There was a window of opportunity – a chance of meaningful intervention – an historic moment ..." But her thoughts were abruptly cut off as she was ejected from the narrative.)

"A central question remains," interrupted the nonconformist clergyman crouched behind the wing chair. "In the case of the infantile disorder of left-wing communism among the Germans, Lenin remarked that the disorder 'has now come to the surface' and that 'The illness does not involve any danger, and after it the body becomes even stronger' – an unmistak-eable allusion to *lichen urticatus,* which requires little more than maintaining regularity of the bowels and a sponging down of the affected parts with bicarbonate of soda dissolved in lukewarm water. But given Lenin's profound personal knowledge of infantile disorder, which particular malady did he have in mind when he subjected Miss Pankhurst to the fire of his rhetoric?"

The clergyman was wearing a black hat, baggy trousers, a white tie, an ingratiating smile and a general look of peering and benevolent curiosity appropriate to a personage poss-essing the complete recordings of Loudon Wainwright III. Inkpin was a little surprised by the clergyman's interruption, and found himself wondering (for reasons available only in the penultimate draft of this story) if he was called Zabci or Zabludow or Zambakides or Zanettos or Zarback or Zwart.

"Did he mean convulsions caused by some weakness of the nerve cells, probably inherited from the Blank side of the family?" the clergyman continued. "Was it a disorder resulting from a meal of coconut or unripe fruit? Did it involve the delicate question of an adherent foreskin? Whatever the nature of the disorder the crucial point is that Lenin did NOT recommend frequent hot packs for the relief of pain and spasm! Instead he urged *flexible tactics*."

"Flexible tactics!" guffawed Inkpin. "My parents tried flexible tactics on me. A fat lot of good it did them! Many are the nights my mother wept in the bathroom while I sprawled upon a pillow, howling piteously while surreptitiously reading *The Life and Opinions of Tristram Shandy* over my father's shoulder. None of their ploys muted me. I declined to be consoled by tinkly Mozart, magisterial Beethoven or soporific Bach (if I wanted anything it was something jaunty and impertinent, like Cardew's immortal "Smash! Smash! Smash the Social Contract!"). The risible tape they used to play beside my cot, which purported to reproduce the allegedly soothing internal thumpings and squelchings of the womb but which sounded more like the disturbed innards of an aged washing-machine, merely aggravated my restlessness. My father sang to me. I vomited with great precision down his nightshirt. My mother sobbed and developed a greenish face. I screamed with laughter. Later we moved to Wales. It rained ceaselessly. Now, tell me, have I got the job?"

"No," said Mme Augarde.

Inkpin rose from his seat, then realised it was an inappropriate moment to engage in levitation. He quickly returned to his chair, after which, putting on a rather exaggerated display of muscle-movements, he stood up.

Saying nothing, he left.

A Rag

Darkness, the sound of rain. An alarm goes off, stops. Darkness, rain bucketing down in the street, muffled noise of traffic, the sounds of someone getting out of bed. A grey glimmer where the heavy velveteen curtains don't meet at the top, a vague nude figure moving in the dark room. Outside the rain easing, a low soft hiss against the leaf-strewn footway, the street cleaners arriving in the dark street, scraps of shouts, the whirr-roar of the mechanised sweeper, the softer brushwork of the sweepers, rattle of a broken can, rags, old bones spilled from a split sack, dark figures gone by daylight.

It is early morning in London, in London, in London, and it begins, the story begins again, it picks up in the darkness where it left off, the rain still falling.

What story?

The story of the fall of rain, of the falling rain, of the rain crashing on the thin bathroom roof, of the rain tick-tocking in the dark leaky loft and tap-tapping on the ceilings and knock-knocking at the door and slivering down panes and blurring the shapes of things, the story of the mound of refuse and the yellowing cast-down cherry tree, the story of the sweepings of a street and the white puddles forming on a lawn, stories of the rain and the wind, old kettles, old bottles, rain soaking through your clothes, the story of rain beating down on a white cottage beside a river, of rain beating down on a grey cottage beside a brook, of rain on old stones and old bones and empty lawns, of rain blowing across empty fields, turbulent down brown dirty gutters, washing the blue-grey shining empty roads.

It is early morning in London. Cut to the rain sweeping across the deserted park; cut to the rain splashing down on the empty tennis court.

Cut to Bodkins reaching for *Halliwell's Film Guide* (and how Bodkins hates Halliwell, who never likes what he likes). The cover: flushed Marilyn in an ultramarine fifties bathing suit and ludicrous high heels, the fingers of her left hand splayed across the upper reaches of her thigh, a solitary little finger and perhaps the ghost of another peeking round the line of her right thigh, posed to display to best advantage the tight twin curves of her taut, bulging rump, her left breast obliterated by the letter L in FILM but recurring un-obliterated on the back cover, a breast which swerves out and up at a strange unreal ninety degree angle, her smile presumably intended to evoke a cheery *well-hi-there!* and *hey-you!* grin and maybe even a *boy-I-could-really-do-with-a-good-fuckin'-from-you-mister!* but which, when you look more closely, seems bleak and cheerless and posed as if what she was really thinking was *shit-I'm-freezing-in-this-dumbass-swimsuit* and/or *Christ-but-I-need-a-drink,* the wrinkles spreading upwards from her left elbow the wrinkles of the time when face and breasts begin to collapse, Halliwell not letting Bodkins' expectations down with his fatuous *Agreeable to look at for those who can stifle their irritation at the non-plot and non-characters*, with Steven H. Scheuer's *Movies on TV* ("Viewers may find the story baffling") almost in the same league.

Two nights earlier Bodkins dreams of the park, of the magic mysterious enticing park, of the crumbling boarded-up buildings by the park gate, of the pathway leading through a dense, luminous forest with an emerald interior crammed with trees reminiscent of the long-limbed ones in *Jurassic Park*, a forest he chooses to ignore as he hurries on, upward, to the meadow, now no longer like the one in either the movie or Maryon Park as it is today, a big, curving bowl of tree-lined grass, containing ghostly figures who involve him in startling, colourful and tightly plotted dream adventures worthy of an opium-fired collaboration between Wilkie Collins and Tolstoy, but which disintegrate into a collage of maddeningly vague fast-thawing scraps as Bodkins' hand punches through the fabric's bright colours, reaching out to silence the alarm. Silencing it, silencing it, and, amid the collapsing scenery, amid the elasticated, evaporating figures hearing again the rain sleeting down into the street, slapping against the pane, tick-tocking in the dark leaky loft and tap-tapping on the ceilings, knock-knocking at the door, a sour taste in your mouth, head aching, empty wine glass on the desk.

Hearing again the rain sleeting down into the street, slapping against the pane, tick-tocking in the dark leaky loft and tap-tapping on the ceilings, knock-knocking at the door, and it begins, the story begins again, it picks up in the darkness where it left off, the rain still falling, the story of the fall of rain, of rain on empty lawns and blowing across empty fields, turbulent down dirty gutters, washing the blue-grey shining empty roads, and all the while (cut to Bodkins in a crowded, smoky bar) a sweet, slow-slow mamba throbbing through the sun-baked emptiness of Tongue (cut to Tongue; cut to Bodkins happy as the grass was green), a vague nude figure moving in the dark room, (cut to a naked figure holding a telephone; cut to the rain sweeping across the deserted park; cut to the rain splashing down on the empty tennis court; cut to the slow-moving crowd on London Bridge), rain pouring down on the empty park and the deserted courts, heart-mysteries there, Martin Stephenson singing "Rain", luminous raindrops suspended from the netting, Leonard Cohen singing "Last Year's Man", green memories cooked to grey rags inside a spreading sabbath desolation, desolate as St Neots, wet as that black shiny childhood day his mother and father, waiting for a long connection, took him to see *Reach for the Sky*, the rain avalanching on the cinema roof, cold as that far seaside winter when her mother died, story upon story, enfolded in rain, sodden with it, and later, on West 10th, going to see *Five Easy Pieces*, going to see *Dead of Night,* going to see *Journey through the Past,* going to see *Don't Look Now*, the rain coming down on Glanville, the rain coming down on Chinatown, the rain coming down on Seattle, rags, tatters without catharsis and still continuing, yes, endlessly in the soft rain, still continuing as Bodmer Bodkins, rag picker and Engels specialist, shabby prestidigitator, amateur photographer, walks across London Bridge heading for the station, a train to Woolwich Dockyard, on his way to Maryon Park, *the magic park*, and as the trains come and go a sweet, pain-gorged slow-slow mamba still plays slow inside the slow, still falling rain.

It is early morning in London. Cut to the rain sweeping across the deserted park; cut to the rain splashing down on the empty tennis court; cut to the slow-moving crowd on London Bridge, every face coated in white paste; cut to Bodkins hurrying along a rainswept urban street, his head obscured by a large black umbrella; cut to young men and women with painted faces running across a wilderness of mud and shattered trees; cut to Bodkins staring at a screen; cut to Bodkins reading Cortázar; cut to Bodkins by a window, looking out at the rain; cut to the young men and women swarming over a yellow bulldozer; cut to Bodkins on the telephone; cut to Bodkins using the rewind button and then the still button; cut to Bodkins listening to *The Future*; cut to running men in yellow coats each bearing the label SECURITY; cut to Bodkins sat by a keyboard; cut to Bodkins at London Bridge station, watching his yellowish ghost in the glass frame of an advert cabinet (sunlit beach scene, woman reclining in blue one-piece bathing costume against an arc of deserted custard yellow sand) which reflects, palely, in the mirror of an adjacent scarlet weighing machine, and again, a misty backdrop of barely decipherable lines, in the big gold vanity mirror of the Italian woman standing by the gate to Platform 12, a frown on her face as she absently applies a rich ruby shade to her thin lips and stares upward at the blank departures board, her mind far from that day seventeen years earlier when she sat on a stool in the bar of the village near Valdagno and the man, ordering his second beer, casually asked her her name.

Rain pouring down on the dark empty park and the deserted courts, grey raindrops suspended from the netting, the rain easing, a low soft hiss against the leaf-strewn pathways, the street cleaners arriving in the dark adjacent streets, scraps of shouts, the whirr-roar of the mechanised sweeper, the softer brushwork of the sweepers, rattle of a broken can, rags, old bones spilled from a split sack, dark figures gone by daylight.

Caro Antonioni... Cut to a train pulling out of London Bridge station; cut to an old man lying in a narrow bed; cut to rain slivering down a pane; cut to Bodkins, motionless by a keyboard; cut to a blank screen. Darkness, the sound of rain. An alarm goes off, stops. Darkness. Nothing happens; no one gets out of bed; there is no one there. Sound of a bulldozer tearing up a tree by the roots; sound of something smashing through a brick wall. Cut to rain pouring down on a waste of shattered trees, mud, caterpillar tracks. Cut to a blank screen, two thin white lines framing a black rectangle, the lines ruptured in the lower right corner by the words BLOW-UP.DOC. Long shot of Bodmer Bodkins standing on a patch of bare grass by two tennis courts; close-up of his face, a nervous half-smile; long shot of a man fading away leaving a rectangle of grass, the green disfigured by darker blotches of weed.

Cut to Bodkins in a phone booth; cut to Bodkins sitting on the floor, telephone in hand, frowning. The lack, the lack of information, the difficulty of getting through to British Rail, phone 071-928-5100 for services to East Anglia, Essex, Southern England, North East, East and South London, beep-beep-beep-beep-beep, beep-beep-beep, forever engaged until, finally, after several days of trying, you get through and learn that on weekday mornings there are four trains an hour from London Bridge, one departing at seven minutes past the hour arriving at Woolwich Dockyard at twenty-five minutes past the hour, one at twenty-one minutes past arriving at thirty-nine minutes past, one at thirty-seven minutes past arriving at fifty-five minutes past and one at fifty-one minutes past arriving at nine minutes past, and then, days later, when you get there, you find that the electronic departures board has a malfunction, that the timetables don't identify the platforms so that, ticket in hand, you walk briskly to and fro across the crowded concourse, you wander from platform to platform, no BR staff anywhere, no one able to answer your question, up and down stone corridors, the electronic departure signboards frozen on every platform, no one you ask knowing where the train to Woolwich Dockyard goes from, until, in the end, in desperation, you go to the ticket office and join the long queue at information/reservations and, later, learn that the train you want is leaving Platform Four at 9.51, and you hurry off, and wait, and wait, and at 9.58 it pulls in and you board and you're on your way, seeing the far aerial on the hilltop, seeing the wastes of south-east London, seeing the grotesque monolith capped by a winking pyramid, pulling in to Deptford, glancing at your *London A-Z*, trying to locate the church where Marlowe's dead body was taken, failing to spot it, the train moving on, arriving at Charlton, your pulse beginning to quicken, wondering if (as the map seems to indicate) the line goes high over the park with a view of the courts, but no, Bodkins is plunged into darkness, into a tunnel and a deep cutting where whirled greenery and dark branches race across the grey sky, and a high grey wall encloses you as the train slows, and I flick back the door lock and step down onto the deserted platform.

Woolwich D-D-D-D-D-Dockyard, d-d-d-d-d-dereliction, d-d-d-d-d-d-decay, drear as d-d-d-d-d-death, dismal, d-d-d-d-d-deadly, dying, dying and out across a f-f-f-f-f-footbridge, down steps, nervy and a little anxious, a prickling sense of unease, along a short boarded-up corridor, out into the fresh air, desolation, an empty street, the narrow footway lined with wooden bollards, turn right for the royal dockyard, the great brick chimney still there, dark and stained with age, the chimney you glimpse as Thomas reaches the strange blue building on the corner and steers the Silver Cloud right, cruising alongside a new housing estate, the buildings at once familiar to Bodkins as he hurries along cheerless Woolwich Church Street, a confetti litter of broken glass on the pavement, the traffic on the dual carriageway racing by at speed, but the blue building's not there, you pictured it probably-no-longer-blue but it's not there at all, it's gone, obliterated by the developers, and there's roadworks at the entrance to Cleveley Close, as you turn sharp left, guessing that this is the little quiet street in the film, the place with the antique shop on the corner, and there ahead of you, yes, *the magic park*, the familiar-from-fifty-viewings park entrance, the environs changed, everything else around here different, everything else wiped from existence at some time during these past twenty-seven years but the park entrance the same, and he walks towards it, stepping in through the open gateway, Colour by Metrocolor and a cold October breeze, pulse thudding, camera loaded and ready, the leaves rustling, still there the four big trees bifurcating the circle of asphalt, still there (and how pleased he is about those trees) (how Bodkins never tires of that sinister, magical shot, Thomas's casual stroll into the mysterious park, the four trees waiting like sentinels, the breeze rustling a foregrounded branch, the sense of someone looking down on Thomas), the queer-looking plump dressed-in-black park-keeper stabbing at litter with his pointed stick, pigeons gathered on the open grass beyond the courts, and Bodkins moving along the path, seeing no one, dense foliage on every side, yellow and amber leaves in thick drifts everywhere, comes to the point where the pathway splits, and following Thomas turns to mount the familiar stepped pathway to the low rise and the opening, mounting with beating heart, camera loaded and at the ready, emerging into the sinister meadow, the picket fence completely gone (not quite: a final half-fallen section of eleven sticks and two posts still there), and the two trees still there, the meadow narrower than you imagined but also longer, the grass not mown and kempt as in the film but thick and wild, and Bodkins loiters by the trees and starts – clack, clack – to take photographs, unnerved by the absence of people, the strange concealing wildness of this park, and now Bodkins knows better, Bodkins, who always used to think it was implausible, a murder in an English park, a body lying there all day under a bushy tree, not noticed by anyone, now he knows better, nothing more plausible than an assassination in this lonely place, hedged in on all sides by dense concealing foliage, concealing branches, flickering leaves, the director never returning to the park, a fragment of his gone life, blasted by a stroke in 1985, born 1912, fifty-four when *Blow-Up* was released, a middle aged man's film, yet present in the furrowed grasses, the pale sky,

41

the hooded ominous deathly casual nothingness, the absences, the director now an old man, speechless, living in Rome perhaps, Ferrara, Verona, don't know, resting in an armchair, perhaps in bed, perhaps at that very moment as you walk to the end of the meadow and back again, trying to work out where the tree was, the tree with the corpse behind it, the tree gone, and another one at the far end a neat sawn stump and a third tree gone down at the foot of the stepped path, a bigger stump with a curious grey-white fungoid growth of overlapping circles spreading across the huddled circle of the long years, twenty-seven years gone like yesterday, gone with the tides of turning time, gone with the draining rain, gone with those bleeding blue lines on that scrap of paper shot down a foaming gutter and lost amidst a low soft hiss against the fouled kerbs and the leaf-strewn pathways, the street cleaners arriving in the nearby streets, shouts and laughter, the whirr-roar of the mechanised sweeper, the softer brushwork of the sweepers, rattle of a broken can, rags, old bones spilled from a split sack, dark figures gone by daylight.

It is early morning in London, in London, in London, and it begins, the story begins again, it picks up in the darkness where it left off, the rain still falling.

What story?

The story of how the trees were cut down at Cambridge Park. The story of Bodkins walking through a waste of mud and shattered branches, taking photographs. The story of the rag-and-bone shop, the absent woman, the records of Hawaiian music. The story of the M11 link road. The story of 111 minutes coming to an end. The story of Bodkins leaving the park, catching the train back to London Bridge. The story of Bodkins' disappearance (long shot of Bodmer Bodkins standing on a patch of bare grass by two tennis courts; close-up of his face, a nervous half-smile; long shot of a man fading away before your eyes, of a rectangle of grass, the green disfigured by darker blotches of weed). The story, say, by the suicide, Pavese. The story of how Clelia, sorrowful and sour, waits to see her treacherous lover for the long last time at the drear station, not seeing him, not seeing him hiding behind the kiosk like a louse, and so the train departs, departs with Clelia at a window, and a sweet, pain-gorged slow-slow mamba plays slow, slow, slow as rain going drip-drip-drip might go, goes, from gutters or inside a damp-smelling loft of cobwebs and darkness.

Darkness, the sound of rain. Extinguished in this night, the blue, the red gold, as Bodkins' hand punches through the fabric's bright colours, the obscurities, the heart-mysteries, a hand with slender fingers reaching out to silence the alarm, terminating a dream, a dream where a low, embedded voice slyly whispers of old iron, old bones, old rags, a dream where rain drifts across a desolate park and malicious gusts whisper obscurely *Dein roter Mund besiegelte des Freundes Umnacht-ung*, or maddeningly *Denkt die nahe Stille Vergessenes, erloschene Engel*, until terminated abruptly by a hand reaching out. Silenced, the scenery collapsing, the elasticated, evaporating figures fast vanishing, hearing again the rain sleeting down into the street, slapping against the pane, tick-tocking in the dark leaky loft and tap-tapping on the ceilings, knock-knocking at the door, a sour taste in your mouth, head aching, empty wine glass on the desk.

It begins again, the rain sleeting down into the street, slapping against the pane, tick-tocking in the dark leaky loft and tap-tapping on the ceilings, knock-knocking at the door, and it begins, the story begins again, it picks up in the darkness where it left off, rain pouring down on the dark empty park and the deserted courts, grey raindrops suspended from the netting, the rain easing, long shot of Bodmer Bodkins standing on a patch of bare grass by two tennis courts, close-up of his face, a nervous half-smile, long shot of a man fading away leaving a rectangle of grass, the green disfigured by darker blotches of weed, a low soft hiss against the leaf-strewn pathways, the street cleaners arriving in the dark adjacent streets, leaving you in the end at the end where you began, amid darkness and the sound of rain.

Pook Tuncks

Tuncks is a good name.
Gerard Manley Tuncks. Pook Tuncks.
The Journals and Papers of Gerard Manley Hopkins (1959)

1

The day ends in smoke. The day ends in smoke 'n' murk and smoulderings and ruins and silence. Dull grey-blue haze over the city against ominous far ruby slab o' sky & everywhere that pungent gunpowdery reek as if it was a cloudy English city dawn on the 6th November 'stead 'o Paris 'n the evenin' o' 21st May.

Pook Tuncks the Englishman dodges dips & runs up the dark alley 'n' through the shinin' open doorways out o' that smoky black 'n' bloody place with everythin' congealin'. Runs from what began in a hundred luminous centres and shone and grew and was quenched, blotted, obliterated. Runs heart poundin' & holding on tight to that trusty journal. Journal in which he entrusts whatever's worth writin' down. Scrawny lines. Words unusual, obscure. Rosacea, for example. Roquelaure. Fike. Figulate. Get back to the raw beginning of things. Plus reflections. Doubt's complicated trap-doors. What's worth rememberin' 'n' what's almost not.

Like masquerades 'n' harlequinades 'n' the broken men of Empire. Like the calumnies which fructify. Like your pallid father's moustache. Like the day endin' in smoke.

Like hidin' out overnight 'n' witnessing what happened next. What happened next. Then getting away. Gettin' back to where you came from. Broken. In despair. In retreat. In full flight from the horror of it all. Survivin'. Enduring. Just as he once wrote, long before it all happened. *I cease the mourning and the abject fast, and rise and go about my works again.* Searching to forget. Needin' some other way. Glimmerings in an abattoir blackness.

Pook Tuncks, the Englishman! Pook Tuncks who was there in the crowd – Paris, January 1871 – when the drummers marched past, and the standard-bearers, and the sombre battalions. I

Pook Tuncks (1844-1889) who took the red flag and climbed the cupola, fixing it WILD CHEERING to the hand of the statue of Liberty.

History, like a life, straightens out in retro. In the middle it's muddle and smoke. The Prussians entered Paris on 1st March 1871. Black flags hung from the houses, the streets deserted. The shops closed, the fountains switched off. The statues of the Place de la Concorde draped. The street lamps not lit at night.

What on planet earth was Pook Tuncks doing there, far from orbit of home, waving an inflammatory scarlet flag, speaking immaculate French? You had no idea, had you?

Succumb to sleek, titillating symmetry and the life of Pook Tuncks is quartered by childhood, the years of restlessness, the Paris days, the eighteen-years-long aftermath.

His childhood.

Vast interesting melting-away garden where Pook giggles and gurgles and wanders amid bright sunlight among staring sunflowers and jiggly butterflies, exploring shady billowing jungles with inquisitive stained fingers, forever green immensities where he arranges his wooden soldiers and re-runs Waterloo while plump invisible acrobats and striped-shirted clowns swing and swell from the overhead washing-line 'n' faraway ice-cream clouds file merrily across an always blue sky. Then a cold, heavy force pushed him through the sun-bronzed door in the old brick wall and he found himself in a grey labyrinth of corridors and draughty classrooms, obliged to huddle at a desk with forty fellow inmates, while a variety of frothy, deranged, frog-eyed, horse-faced authoritarian misfits spat mathematics at him, dull salvoes of Latin and spiky Greek, and the cold, iron pellets known as Principles of Religion.

His mother. A sour, constipated old wretch in the photographs, clinging to a chair to steady herself in a turbulent &

uncertain world. Spick and span was her motto. Cleanliness is next to etc. Pook remembers her vaguely. A kindly face who bobbed hither 'n' thither about the house. Sometimes irascible, often peevish and shouty to the servants, on the whole beaming and motherly. Enjoyed the fiction of Charles Kingsley. Strangled to death on a bedsheet, aged thirty-seven, had she been drinking?

Pook's brothers and sisters – Cyril, Art, Everard, Lionel, Millicent, Kate and Grace – are forgettable and forgotten. Call them graceless, call them a dismal, pious, undistinguished crew, paddling the narrow bum-boat of life down the sluggish ditch of their destiny. Dark, yawning offices, black accounts books, embroidery, immense spinsterhoods & bachelorhoods, tiny nothingnesses gobbling up the yellowed long uneventful years. Pook had little to do with them once they all left home.

His father, Manfred. Big in the small world of marine insurance. A very successful average adjuster, an admirable fellow. Hand on hip, fingers of his right hand showing off his gold watch, tick tock. Punctuality, a hard day's work, no slacking. A split infinitive put him out of sorts for the week. Kept stick-insects in a jar, a servant dealt with the excreta. Fished for sticklebacks and pike. Wrote a paper about a giant dragonfly he saw fluttering past Nugent's Cranny. Collected cutlery from eighteenth-century Venice. Was very attentive towards his moustache. Permitted it to obscure – just – his lower lip. Always trimming it carefully to evade the appellation *walrus*. Made the consumption of soup a living nightmare but nothing a good soaking in water and a brisk towelling couldn't cleanse. Eh? Combed his hair sideways to cope with baldness. Weak, watery eyes. What happened to Pook broke his businessman's heart.

3

What happened to Pook.

After leaving home: the years of restlessness.

Incredibly, Pook showed little interest in the family business.

When his father mentioned the heady challenges and aesthetic rewards of marine insurance Pook had the rudeness to yawn. He twitched. Fidgeted. Drifted off. His parents blamed Balliol. Higher education can be a very dangerous thing. It makes young people dissatisfied with marine insurance and banking. It gives them notions. Balliol gave Pook notions he had not engendered when at hearth and home.

To name just one, the idea of becoming a painter. As if the world wasn't groaning at the seams with paintings! As if the cities of the world weren't littered with galleries already chockfull of Madonnas and shameless nudes and stags at bay and views of the heath in stormy weather.

Balliol marked the beginning of the restless years. The years of beginning to formulate a *Weltanschauung,* not an easy thing for some people. Why has God squeezed us by muscular contractions and repellent lubrication out of this particular womb? Why did God select this particular narrow-minded biped to lurk smirking beside the cot? Where Do We Come From? What Are We? Where Are We Going?

When you leave home you start to learn about Things. For example, the episode when the policeman with the handlebar moustache stopped him at midnight and asked him his name and he said "Pook Tuncks", whereupon the policeman hit him hard in the thorax with his baton, dragged him off in handcuffs to the station and charged him with (i) being drunk and disorderly, (ii) offensive behaviour, (iii) uttering a lewd and insulting remark to a member of the Metropolitan Police. A misunderstanding only cleared up when Mr Tuncks pulled various gold and silver strings and personally assured the Commissioner of his son's tee-totalling zeal.

Which was not strictly true, Pook having developed at Oxford a passion for wines both fortified and unfortified.

Pook made many drawings and watercolours and then abandoned his dream of becoming a painter. He knew he would never be as good as George Frederick Watts. But poetry, that was something different. He rather thought at a push he could do better than Tennyson.

Furtively, alone in his room, he spurted lines, jotted and scribbled ecstatically. Old habits die hard, and he continued the practice until paralysis overtook his fingers a mere forty-eight hours before the big sleep.

An early sample.

Look! Look!
My name is Pook!
Pook Tuncks!
Not a cab-driver, Carthaginian, Christ-mad collector of cruc-
    ifixes, crisp cryer of cabbages, one of those drunks
you see in doorways, no!
I am Pook
the poet,
blue-eyed watcher o' the sparrow's beak, the heron's wings
and cauliflower clouds, and jagged amber leaves, and
jigs 'n' reels 'n' things.

Those who only knew Pook Tuncks as a rumpled, morose, balding, middle-aged mumbler with whisky on his breath and gravemarkers on his hands and purply blotches on his face and neck, and all the energy and fun snuffed out of him, would never have believed he was once buoyant and frisky, given to constant erections and frequent versification, with a flawless, boyish complexion and long, dark, shining hair of a kind truly remarkable in the pre-shampoo era. At Balliol he could juggle five satsumas at once; his trick with a pineapple and elastic was stupefying; unforgettable his unusual balancing of a flute of port. His ability to mimic both trombone and harmonica and give a lively performance of the Goldberg Variations in the style of Pujol astounded and delighted everyone who heard him.

Two days after matriculating, Pook could be seen beside the Cherwell, gesticulating. The reason for it has been lost. In the weeks that followed he constantly skulled. When no one was watching he began to munch boats, confiding to his Journal, *I know nothing so luxuriously delicious as a canoe.*

Forgetting that his father had devoted his life to marine matters, Pook wrote him a poignant letter omitting his more interesting exploits in order to explain that *A canoe is a long light covered boat, the same shape both ways, with an opening in the middle where you recline, with your feet against one board, your back against a cushion on another.*

His father, who had recently become interested in cushions, wrote back requesting more information about the sort used in canoes. Pook's reply has been lost.

Rugby football , cricket, tennis, racquets and fives – there is no evidence that Pook had the slightest interest in any of these absurd sports. He much preferred walking, winking, dunking, nudism and astronomy.

In the long vacation of 1863 Pook holidayed on the Isle of Wight, observing it to be *diamond-shaped, with many high cliffs.* Interviewed in 1901, his landlady, Mrs Grubber, had no recollection of Tuncks. "I used to have so many young gentlemen staying," she explained, a cheerful flush on her ballooning cheeks.

It was around this time that Pook experimented with flagellation and fasting. He began to wear chasubles and a wire girdle, for prickly thrills. The girdle consisted of linked hoops which adjusted to crush his breast, squeeze his ribs and nip playfully the swell of upper buttock.

Pook even genuflected two or three times, but soon gave it up, worried about becoming insane. Haberdashery soothed him for a fortnight. On 21 January 1866 Pook stopped taking sugar in his tea. He made a vow – broken on Ascension Day – never again to eat pudding on Sundays. That summer he climbed Glastonbury Tor and wrote a demented tract (now lost) which argued that Christ had been condemned by the Mayor of Shepton Mallet, and that the Tor was the authentic site of Golgotha. When Pook arrived home in Hampstead his father told him to wash the dirt off his face – his jocular, brutish way of acknowledging Pook's attempted moustache.

In 1867 Pook obtained his degree and left Balliol. The second week of July he journeyed to Paris with Basil, a Russian admiral's son. For seven days they sightsaw (Notre Dame, Mona Lisa, Seine trip, Bois de Boulogne) then returned to England via Bayeux and Dieppe. Little did he think that one day –

For the rest of the summer Pook visited his grandparents, his aunts and his uncles, and in September he started work as a schoolmaster in Edgbaston. He obtained lodgings on Deacon Street with a Polish tea merchant's widow. *Fancy me getting up at a quarter past six!* he wrote in his Diary.

Pook was deeply depressed over the next ten months . How he hated schoolteaching! How he hated the ignorant, snickering louts he was expected to teach! How he loathed the curriculum! How he would much rather have been painting allegorical canvases or writing collections of poems which sold by the tens of thousands!

The summer of 1867 could not come too quickly. Pook headed for Switzerland and had a very enjoyable time. In Basel he met Wilberforce, a fanatical Brontëan, who had recently made a pilgrimage to Charlotte Brontë's school in Brussels. In Lauterbrunnen he met a man who claimed that Australia was made out of barley sugar. Near Zurich he heard two jockers yodelling. In Montreux his attention focussed on a strange party of Americans. In the mountains he witnessed a girl with spindle and distaff, manipulating dairy cattle. Upon his return to England Tuncks visited the National Gallery. He asked a deaf attendant named Watt if there was a Watts on show, but the man looked perplexed and would only say, "What? What? What?"

The period September 1868 to December 1870 passed in a frenzy of copulation between young Pook and Maria Zelcowicz, his merry, sparkly-eyed, thirty-nine year-old landlady. Pook, who, up until then, had no experience of women, found the experience enormously invigorating. He began to drink to excess, vomit, have hangovers, get in late for work and make risqué jokes about Queen Victoria.

On February 14th 1871 a tearful Maria told an astounded Pook that their affair was over. She had fallen in love with a transvestite hippopotamus-impersonator from Penge. His name was Rudolph. He wore make-up and intriguing under-garments, and was sexy in a way Pook would never be. Pook gasped and did something he hadn't done for years. Adopting a crouching position, he flabbergasted Maria with an angry, passionate trombone performance of the Overture to *The Magic Flute*. But, though enormously impressed, Maria knew that ingenious, melodious gusts alone were not enough to reconstruct the broken spans and shattered timbers of the collapsed structure of their love.

Untrue, of course. There was no impersonator. It just fizzled out, the way it often does. Maria returned to stone and it was time to move on.

Heartbroken, Pook resigned his job. He packed his Journal, his unpublished verses and his wire-girdle, and headed for Paris.

4

Pook had notions of slumping on a cot in a high, gloomy garret, occasionally dipping his primitive pen into a sloppy ink-pot and scratching out some splattery rhyming couplets mourning his lost love, an activity punctuated by trips to the window to gaze down at the romantic Seine, its windswept embankments and the ubiquitous, nauseating, hugging, entranced, deliriously happy lovers.

No such luck. His lodgings near the Boulevard Voltaire were on the ground floor and faced a sooty factory with clattering innards. The factory manufactured Gulliver Bolts for the aerostat industry. Pook's bed was large and comfortable. Toast, pancakes, raspberry jam and cheap red wine sapped his creative juices. He slumped, snoozed and was unable to write a line.

Did I say he thrust a red flag into Liberty's hand? Can't see Pook doing a thing like that, must have been someone else. And his French wasn't immaculate, either. It was OK, it got him by, but that was all.

What Pook was aware of.

(i) The weather. Not bad for that time of year.

(ii) His misery. Unrelenting. Maria's naked form stretched out enticingly upon his bed, her slender arms reaching out to pull him down. But when his fingers touched hers she vanished in a flash, and disappeared , screeching and fiery, exactly like the witch in *Conan the Barbarian*.

(iii) Paris. There seemed to be quite a lot of fuss about something.

Of what did this fuss consist?

Thunder. Booms in the distance.

People shouting.

Screams.

Pistol shots, rifle-fire.

Long processions filing along the main boulevards. And such-like.

Pook was vaguely aware there had recently been a war between Prussia and France (which the Prussians had won). But what the new fuss was all about he really had no idea. It began on 18th March when he went out for a stroll and en-countered the streets full of excited crowds, artillerymen and cannon. Some people were busily taking up paving stones and constructing barricades. A General swaggered past, clanking, looking very red in the face and upset. Drums thudded urgently; musket-fire crackled nearby. Soldiers and crowds swirled around the Hôtel de Ville.

Next morning Pook learned that the Government had evaporated. The red flag flew over the Hôtel. The Ministers, the administrators, the chiefs of this and the chiefs of that, the mayors and deputies, the functionaries, were fleeing to Versailles. The Ministries were being cleared. Columns of government troops marched off through the gates of the Left Bank. Schools, hospitals, justice, the police – all left to the citizens of Paris!

"We must first march on Versailles, disperse the Assembly and appeal to la France!" cried someone. A call which went unheard. A call stifled by habit, custom, legality, all the old stale dead traditions which weigh down on human minds. The Central Committee neglecting to shut the gates. The Central Committee concerning itself with holding an election. The Committee not seeing that it faced a death-struggle with the Assembly of Versailles. Not comprehending the phenomenon of Dual Power. The Central Committee a mish-mash of forces, lacking a coherent programme.

The days fatally passing in muddle and delay. Pook Tuncks attempting conversations, trying to get hold of English newspapers. Learning the meaning of *incalescent* and *quaestuary* and *fitz*.

Sunday 26th March, a gorgeous crisp sunlit day, sky all blue, Pook stayed in bed until eleven, hot thoughts of Maria making him tremble and sweat. Took a day trip to Versailles to see what was happening there, soon forgot her, found the station full of belligerent gendarmes, who snapped at him for his passport but were nice as pie once they discovered Mr Tuncks was an English gentleman. Could hardly help but notice the contrast between V – gloomy sullen streets, cowed people with bruised faces being dragged along to prison by scowling gendarmes – and P. Hurly-burly streets of the capital aswarm with people, wall-posters everywhere describing the attacks, the defence, the latest news, posters of the Central Committee, and the cafés packed and noisy.

The elections! The results! 200,000 Parisians outside the Hôtel de Ville, the battalion drums beating, red fringes round their muskets, banners, soldiers of the line, artillerymen and marines, long red streamers hanging from buildings, the bayonets piled in a heap, bright sunshine glittering and flashing on the blades, tricolours, red tassels, three cheers, hurrah, people singing, a band playing the *Marseillaise* and then the *Chant du Depart*, trumpets sounding a charge, the cannon thundering on the quay, glorious, unforgettable, what a day!

The noise subsides. The members of the Central Committee and of the Commune appear on the platform, their red scarfs over their shoulders. A member of the Committee announces the names of those elected. The drums beat a salute, two hundred thousand voices break into the *Marseillaise*. Gabriel Ranvier, member of the Commune for the 20th arrondissment, cries out, "In the name of the people, the Commune is proclaimed!"

Thousandfold thunderous roar, "Vive la Commune!" Caps flung up on the ends of bayonets, flags fluttering, ten thousand hands waving handkerchiefs out of windows, from rooftops, cannonboom, drums, bands playing ... And then the lowering of the flags, officers saluting with their sabres , the men raising their muskets.

Bemused, bewildered, exhilarated, astounded, Pook understood little. Knew not that whereas the Central Committee consisted of ordinary people, the Council of the Commune abounded in factions and fractions and infinitesimal coteries, upstarts of yesterday, semi-celebrities, interminable rivalries and squabbles and bickerings. The Council of the Commune thereby abandoned – disaster! – to whims, individual inspiration, giddiness, reformism, moderation, random motions. The Commune without a military plan, without a programme, without general views, indulging itself in interminable, desultory discussions.

And on 2nd April, without warning, at one o'clock, the Versaillese launched their first shells upon Paris.

And the bright weather ended, and a fog came down. A dense clammy penetrating fool-you fog inside which was born shouting, shots, skirmishes, fighting, confusion.

"Surrender and your lives will be spared," General Pellé informed a group of surrounded Communards.

The Parisians surrendered. The Versaillese at once seized the soldiers fighting for the Commune and shot them. Later, the officers were shot. And Emile Duval, member of the Commune for the 13th arrondissement, was shot. And his chief of staff was shot. And the commander of the volunteers of Montrouge was shot. And Pook Tuncks, tucked up in bed, knew nothing of this, though once he thought he heard some distant pops.

5

Miserable triflings, animosities, disputations, paralysis, two-masks men, the weakness – the problem of recall – of delegates elected by geographical area rather than the workplace, the fine and fiery and empty proclamations, the secret, stupefying timidity of certain revolutionary leaders, the legality-mongers, the scenes of tragic farce at the Bank of France: of this Pook knew nothing. All he saw was the unexpected tidiness of the city.

All he saw was the lovers by the Seine, and the children playing, and that whatever it was, it wasn't the end of the world.

He saw the fountains playing in the great squares, wandered into the thrown-open palace. He saw the fire in the eyes of the Communards, felt the sense of liberation, excitement, joy. Newspapers, broadsheets, leaflets bursting out like crocuses in spring, and everywhere you went talk, talk, talk, debate, argument, gesticulations and fervent jabber.

On 6th April – of a sudden he scarcely thought of phantom Maria – at two o'clock in the afternoon, Pook drifted with the multitude, flowed to the Beaujon Hospital. The dead on display in their coffins across the yard. Many, shot after combat, bearing the marks of cords on their arms. Women screaming, wailing, sobbing, bending over the corpses, recognising stone faces with staring eyes, cries of fury, vows of vengeance. Pook shaken; had never before witnessed ... Felt their fury.

You couldn't imagine this sort of thing happening in Edgbaston, or for that matter Westminster.

Could you?

Heart-stopping dead reverberating sound of muffled drums half silencing the misery, the coffins sealed and loaded. Three immense catafalques, each containing thirty-five coffins, covered with black crêpe, decorated with red flags, each drawn by eight horses, slowly rolled towards the great boulevards, preceded by trumpets and the *Vengeurs de Paris*. Behind, the chief mourners. Charles Delescluze, wrinkled delegate for the

19th arrondissement, and five other members of the Commune, bare-headed, red-scarfed. The streaked widows, the silent
baffled children. Followed by thousands upon thousands of
women, children and men, immortelles in their button-holes,
no one saying a word, and everywhere the dead reverberating
sound of the thudding muffled drums.

At intervals passing groups of musicians dressed all in black
who played subdued strains of music. The wind took the music
and twisted it, made it sob and whine, Pook thinking he
recognises the pulsing Andante from "Death and the Maiden",
scraps of the Largo from "Trio des esprits", and other melodies
unknown, impossible, a few slow, stray chords from "Pleasures
of the Harbor" say, or a mournful "Worn Out Blues" with a
drawn-out sax.

At the Père Lachaise wrinkled Delescluze walked towards the
mass grave. Stooped, stared into the raw pit. Perfume of his
own coming extinction coldly brushing against his old face;
salutes the dead. *I will make you no long speeches ... These
have already cost us too dear ...*

What's that?

Pook, straining to understand. Frowning, cupping his hands
over his ears. Consulting his pocket dictionary.

*Justice for the families of the victims! Justice for the great
town which, after five months of siege, betrayed by its
Government, still holds in its hands the future of humanity!
Let us not weep for our brothers who have fallen heroically,
but let us swear to continue their work, and to save Liberty,
the Commune, the Republic!*

Next day the Versaillese shelled the Avenue of Neuilly.

6

It all ends in smoke. The last of all days endin' in smoke 'n'
murk and smoulderings and ruins and silence. Dull grey-blue
haze over the city against ominous far ruby slab o' sky &
everywhere that pungent gunpowdery reek as if it was a cloudy
English city dawn on the 6th November 'stead o' Paris 'n the

evenin' o' 21st May.

Confusion of the Commune turnin' to a shambles. Fog, grapeshot, surprise nocturnal attacks. Fires and smoke along L'Avenue de la Grande Armée ... Porte-Maillot ablaze ... Asnières and Levallois in ruins ... One thousand five hundred shells whistling down upon the people *every day*. The shattered houses of Neuilly ... fragments of shells ... rats ... Munition of the wrong calibre sent to the forts. Panic at Issy, neglected watches. The night of 3rd May at the redoubt of the Moulin Saquet. Issy by this time no longer a fort but shell-battered rubble and earth. Fog, grapeshot, surprise nocturnal attacks. The bourgeoisie – deputies, functionaries, priests, officers, parasol women – gathered together on the heights to watch the shelling of the turbulent proletariat. Everythin' endin' street by street, house by house, in smoke & blood & chaos. The proletariat without direction; without military organisation. A patchy, inefficient defence & the beginning of the nights of horror. Beginnin' o' the end. Perpetual roaring of cannon, bayonets and pistol-shots. Pools of blood glowing in the glimmer of burning houses. Now for the spade and the paving stones! Let the earth be heaped up and mattresses shelter the combatants. "Come, citizen, lend a hand for the Republic!"

At the Bastille tourist Pook saw crowds of workers, some digging the earth, others carrying paving stones; children using spades and mattocks as big as themselves. Girls hacking with heavy pickaxes, sparks showering from the stone. Saw, at the intersection of the Square St. Jacques and the Boulevard Sebastopol the market women, labouring hard, filling earth sacks and wicker baskets. Saw the barricades of May, built of paving stones, hardly as high as Pook. Behind the barricades, sometimes, a cannon or a machine-gun; red flags, drooping.

Walls crumbled by shells and bombs, perforated lions by the broken fountains. Trees leafless blackened stalks. Dust, fire, blazing architecture of arches, cupolas, spectral edifices, sparks & Pook runnin' down the Boulevard Voltaire.

Humid glimmer o' Saturday mornin' & the cold getting to yr

bones. Mute & desolate city. Worn out, wiped out, blood-washed 'n' shot. Forty-two men, three women and four children led to No. 6 in the Rue des Rosiers, forced to kneel bare-headed before the wall, then shot. Including the woman who refused to kneel and held her child in her arms. Forty-nine corpses, walls dripping with brains, total of 200,000 dealt with in this way, flesh-flies swarmin' over the streets in dense dark clouds ... Immense graves of lime, bodies burned with petroleum, prisoners in cattle-wagons.

Pook Tuncks the Englishman dodges, dips & runs up the dark alley 'n' through the shinin' open doorways out o' that smoky black 'n' bloody place with everythin' congealin'. Runs from what began in a hundred luminous centres and shone and grew and was quenched, blotted, obliterated. Rest o' the story easy to tell, back to England & the broken years of despair , the long aftermath 1871-89, every life having its peak & following long decline & emptinesses.

7

Rest o' the story. Eighteen grindin' years o' nothin' much – indigestion, attacks o' dandruff, a spot of mackerel fishing on the Isle of Man. Exploring enormous hard-to-carry dictionaries, writin', scratchin', playin' his organ. Never married, never met another woman like Maria. Once went back wracked to Edgbaston but she'd moved. And the years flowed, and it was cloudy to the end o' the story, rain upon rain, washin' his life away. Pook in his room, reading *The Times,* reading *The Illustrated London News,* reading the mail, receiving the death news. Sniffin' the sweat of his armpits. Poor Basil. (Remember Basil? – trip to Paris, part 3.) Committed suicide, a Greek girl, madly in love, found dead in a pool beside a railway line in France. Another Balliol acquaintance froze to death in a snowstorm in Minnesota. How awful! But he didn't feel a thing. Not after the Commune. Not after what he'd seen from his window. Not after what he'd seen in the street. The brains dripping on walls, the heap upon heap of dead women, dead children. Blotted it out with brandy after brandy. And the dandruff no sooner obliterated than problems with haemorrhoids. Like a cluster of cherries around his anus. Astonishing muscular dexterity and manual encouragement required to get out thin strings o' chipolatas, some of the cherries invariably rupturing and spraying powerful tiny anarchic jets. Fed up of anaemia and of mopping walls and carpet he submitted to a thirty-minute haemorrhoidectomy. Mr Gay and Mr Prance, experts in their field. Pruned the fruit and in no time Pook was up and about, up to his old tricks, brandy-breathed and able once more to scrawl *mofette* without shuddering, blissfully unhindered by mogigraphia. Eighteen long years, working as a General Teacher (Logic; Rhetoric; Greek; Latin; History; Mathematics) in various prep schools. Spink Hill, Liverpool, Glasgow , Wales, awful places like that, places always short of teachers. In the winter of 1878 he suffered from diarrhoea, headache, stomach-ache, earache, temporary deafness, hot flushes and vomiting brought on by the hot weather. In 1879 he went to an exhibition at the Royal Academy to look at paintings by Millais, Walker and Watts. In 1880 he endured phimosis, balanitis and ulceration, necessitating further delicate pruning. The following year, in August, he bought a stout walking stick and explored the Duke of Newcastle's seat at Clumber Park. In 1883 he suffered from several bad headaches. In 1886 he drafted the plan for a book provisionally entitled *A Popular Guide to Light and Ether* but soon gave up trying to write it. In 1887 he had a holiday in Devon, spending a pleasant week in the Lostwithiel area. In 1889, aged forty-five, he died. Typhoid.

His puffy-faced pink-cheeked bluff sporty chump brother Cyril sorted out Pook's things. Glanced at Pook's Journal, eyes bulging to see the squalid scandalous things he'd written about, a disgrace! Would be a dreadful embarrassment to the family if – So quite naturally burned it. Also came across a box full of poems. Some three hundred, numbered. What's this? "The Wreck of the Commune"?

Cubatory proletarians of Paris
Fight on! Stomachous, fight the iron hand o'
Mercenary soldiery and the fedifragous conspirators!
Sthenobulia, my brother or my sister!
Know there is nothing can be quelled by niddering despots blind
Or vengeance o' the police-tinged bourgeois mind;
Know that amid the trucidation and the rain
The stilp battle must break out again!

One glance was enough, Cyril didn't need to read the other thirty-four preposterous stanzas. Burned the lot. But kept the tartan carpet slippers (which fitted perfectly!), the pretty little Cornish pisky plus the runcible spoon and delightful snowstorm paperweight, the splendid brandy glass, the case of four-star V.S.O.P. Cognac, the useful trouser-press and Pook's best pencil sharpener.

The moral. Every story should have one. How about. How about. Something about the cloudy etymology of "Communism"? Tiananmen Square and – Something along the lines of "The people never hold sway but for an hour, and woe to them if they are not then ready"? Something about a breed of Tuncks, of whom only one, our little grey Pook, came anywhere near to –

Something about the witnesses, the humerus bones?

Did I mention he was only four feet eleven inches tall?

Dying, shiverin' Pook remembered how, near the end, the light ceased at the entrance of the Faubourg Montmartre. Stagey thunder, flashes and pops. Strange, yes, how the light ceased there, abruptly, giving it the appearance (now he came to think about it) of an enormous black hole into which the Communards filed and did not return, that night or ever. /

Remembered he had left his girdle behind in Montparnasse!

Offstory

Sleepless at 3am and can't get back. Wide, very wide, awake. Footfalls, fading, in the street. Silence. Distant slam of a car door. Silence. More footsteps, two people. Couple having an argument. *But I do love you. I do.* Silence. *Fuck off, leave me alone.* Footsteps, gone. Silence. *No real sleep*, said the spirit. *That is the price.* We will pay it, we will pay it. We said. Tell us, we said. We want to know. No, said the spirit. Yes, we said. Tell us. Now. Bladder full, must go. Need a paracetamol too. That's better. Back to bed, her warmth. Very wide, the surge rushing in, adrift. An empty beach, sand. Grey dunes. The old shipwreck far out. Rusted iron scraps lodged in the undisturbed sand. Scotland. Off by heart the place of ferns and the place of rocks, the place of fire. Off by heart Bredon Hill in icy December. So bitter cold. The grass gemmed with dew. Leaves silver. Cracked ice on the dented lid of the blue heart-shaped sand tray. The black VW, the blazing headlights. Switch them off, yes. Her fur coat, her long flowery dress. The wastes of shining stars. Long panning shot, brick pillar, iron fence, barbed wire. Derelict buildings, chimneys. Scrap of something flapping on the wire. Sheet of paper? Ragged handkerchief? More scraps. Abandoned, torn clothing. *Now not a soul is here*. Empty. Empty hangars. The control tower. And now. *Derelict.* That hot restless unforgettable summer. Reading *Dead Souls*. Her stockings hanging to dry. Lou Reed. *It's so cold, in Alaska.* "How many years are there?" Asked the seven-year-old. A question I found difficult to answer. Followed by what's called *a pregnant silence*. Silence. Then gave birth to a word: "Lots." *Not satisfied!* Can you believe it? "Yes, but how many?" Managed to continue, managed to muster a beaming, authoritative adult response: "One hundred!" "Thanks." DERELICT, yes. Lodged between DERBYITE ("a recruit who volunteered for service under the scheme originated by the Earl of Derby in 1915") and DERELICTION ("abandonment with an intention not to reclaim"). Not far from DERANGE-MENT and a green sea-fish with a black tail. Same page as a sinking of the spirits and a muscle that draws down the part to which it is attached. DERELICT. Meaning: abandoned. Meaning: a wreck adrift on the open sea. Meaning: anything thrown away, relinquished or abandoned. A tract of land left dry by the sea, and fit for cultivation or use. Empty hangars. No more happy landings. Telephone numbers scribbled on the wall. A pin-up girl ... a name. A sign on the floor. "Goodbye." "Good luck!" "Thanks." *It was very different in* – Can't take much more of this. Boring. Cold. Need a good story. Rounded characters, psychological realism, verisimilitude. Verisimilitude's the ticket. Not this farrago. Failing that, failure. Or success. Pack it all in and begin again. Something altogether different. Earn the OBE for services to British commercial interests in Thailand, say. Or perhaps purchase an aqualung, perhaps get an MBE. There are still services to perform in deep sea research in Bermuda. Or perhaps something to do with animals. A nice shiny honour for services to the pig industry. Or something cold and clean and white and foolish, involving a flag. Services to mountaineering, obviously. Or perhaps (tingling strangely) perhaps purchase a fetching lipstick and various items of women's clothing, soften my voice and apply myself to the work of the Taunton Deane Women's Royal Voluntary Service. Failing all that, a hot bath. A good night's sleep. Sleep on it. Feel better in the morning. Tomorrow is etc. Yes. Hot bath, bed, glass of scotch. On ice. Cracked ice, the injured fields. So bitter cold. The proof of the pudenda is – Under the wastes of shining stars. So bitter cold. Remembering. The old *Love* & *Fame* feelings. The *Songs of Love* & *Hate* time. Stay away from bridges and balconies. Keep the medicine cabinet locked. Stay off the sauce. All other things to their destruction draw. Including our decaying loves. The adding years with their drip-drip-drip of days and nights, the unending rains wearing all away, the fine layers of settling dust, the sudden mudslides. The fog, the hot nights. The sprinkling rain. And the sun went down in flame. So bitter cold. The grass gemmed with dew. Leaves silver. Cracked ice on the dented lid of the blue heart-shaped sand tray. And lost as strangers as we pass. "I'd like you to read this. Not now. Later." Can't take much more of this. Can't take much more of this. Afterwards. The always afterwards, the after words, the weird wires, the wet woods, the lit wards, the winking and the wiles, the wild wheels within wheels. Gave her a volume of Housman's verse. What? When? Really? I'm not sure that I – Can't take much more of this. No. Calm down. Relax. Take it easy. Find a warm beach. Find a good book to read. F. Scott Fitzgerald, HISTORIAS DE PAT HOBBY, say. Or how about D. H. Lawrence, EN EL ERIAL. Or perhaps Suzanne Labin is more your cup of tea: HIPPIES, DROGAS Y SEXO. Or Virginia Woolf, FIN DE VIAJE. Or Doris Lessing, EL CUARDERNO DORADO. Or for something lighter: Mary Westmacott (Agatha Christie), LEJOS DE TI ESTA PRIMAVERA. Prefer poetry, on the whole.

She rais'd my Hopes, and brought them just in view, And then in spight the pleasing Scene withdrew. No. Not spite. Spite's too easy. Something far muddier and more mysterious and less malicious than spite. Heartbroken at Heathrow. Sad eyes. Turning face. The tracks of light, the tracks of light. Yet still I gasping live. Amid the old absurd.

COURT CIRCULAR. 12 November. The Yang di-Pertuan Agong of Malaysia and The Raja Permaisuri Agong of Malaysia, with the Malaysian Suite in attendance, left Buckingham Palace this morning upon the conclusion of the State Visit to The Queen and The Duke of Edinburgh. Sir Kieran Prendergast (British High Commissioner to the Republic of Kenya) and Lady Prendergast were received by The Queen. The Duke of Edinburgh, Member, Driving Awards Committee, Coach Makers and Coach Harness Makers Company, this morning held a meeting at Buckingham Palace. His Royal Highness this afternoon attended a Luncheon given by the Executive Committees of the Army Board at the Officer's Mess, The King's Troop, Royal Horse Artillery, St John's Wood Barracks, London NWS. Brigadier Miles Hunt-

Davis was in attendance. KENSINGTON PALACE 12 November: The Princess of Wales, Colonel-in-Chief, the Light Dragoons, received Colonel Robert ffrench Blake (Colonel of the Regiment), Lieutenant-Colonel Andrew Stewart upon relinquishing his appointment as Commanding Officer and Lieutenant-Colonel Robert Webb-Bowen upon assuming the appointment. *The czar's diary is the best of all testimony. From day to day and from year to year drags along upon its pages the depressing record of spiritual emptiness. "Walked long and killed two crows. Drank tea by daylight." Promenades on foot, rides in a boat. And then again crows, and again tea. The intellectual force of the czarina is not higher, but rather lower than her husband's. Even more than he, she craves the society of simpletons* (Trotsky). Can't take much more of this. Roll on the Revolution. I feel it near, I do, really. Amid the little rubbish of the day's doings I feel the ache and shift and sudden acceleration of the great moving forces of history. The avalanche. The avalanche ghosts. Long overdue. A red gleam amid the grey years, the grey years. Yes, years. The years. Year added to year. A pile of them, like thrown-away carpets. The adding years with their drip-drip-drip of days and nights, the unending rains wearing all away, the fine layers of settling dust, the sudden mudslides. *She looked as if she were telling the truth, though with women, especially blue-eyed women, that doesn't always mean anything.* "Let's listen to the rest of it," I said. "I like details and things." On the night of July 1st 1968 there was heavy rain. The temperature rose. Next morning was boiling hot and everything for miles was coated in a fine film of reddish dust. There was, there is. There was a high of 34°C at Liphook. There is cracked ice on the dented lid of the blue heart-shaped sand tray. Fur coat, flowery dress. The silver wastes. I like details and things.

Off by heart. Offstory. E, tapping on the glass as I walked by, waved, killed, absurdly, by a falling tree. The cloudy sweetly scented room, the Incredible String Band playing "This Moment", J returning the borrowed copy of Loudon Wainwright's first LP, then going off to be killed in a road crash. A got religion and became boring, Marie led me through an underground passage to the elaborate black magic markings on the floor of the derelict building. Tampering with death, asking when Belinda would die. The spirit did not wish to tell us, we made it. We paid the asked-for price. *2007*, said the dead one, and I felt the chill. And slept soundly. Wrote down the date somewhere, hope I still have it. Always meant to check the obituaries that week in 2007, after we lost touch, as we did lose touch, all of us. J died soon after, A got religion. B married a lawyer.

Idea for a story. All of us dying on that same day in 2007. Different locations. Saudi Arabia for L. Somewhere in Wales for A. B in Surrey. Simultaneously, across the time zones. Night, day, dusk. Black BMW careers off the road (no, make it a black VW). Cancer of the liver. Fourteen-inch slate blown off a high Bayswater roof in a storm. House-fire. Steep flight of stone stairs, carelessly abandoned roller-skate. Gas leak. An IRA bomb in a litter bin. Sharp was just passing. Police found the burned remains of a page bearing the words *While I was trying to fix in my mind every detail of this grand landscape, Captain Nemo remained motionless, as if petrified in mute ecstasy, leaning on a mossy stone*. Scotland Yard sleuths have identified the text involved and are currently searching day and night through the Dent/Dutton edition of *20,000 Leagues Under the Sea*, containing a unique "Log of the *Nautilus*" listing all specifically indicated dates and places visited. And? There was, there is. Rags. And bones. And sand. A sandstorm boiling in the Sahara shoots sand up into the atmosphere. The finest grains are sucked up and propelled on a strong southerly, covering 2,800 km in about 40 hours. When the dust reaches Britain it is sometimes washed down from rain-bearing clouds, and thousands of tons are deposited on the ground as a pale beige blanket, often lying unnoticed after rainfall. Very wide, the surge rushing in, adrift. An empty beach, sand. Grey dunes. The old shipwreck far out. Rusted iron scraps lodged in the undisturbed sand. Off by heart. Going to see *Five Easy Pieces*. Going to see *Journey through the*

Past. English Bay, the fireworks. Enough, stop. Get to work on a novel instead. A big one. Six hundred solid pages. Narrative drive. Fascinating characters. Gripping octopuses in exotic locations. The story of Seth Splint. Rags to riches. Interesting dialogue. Chapter Twenty-Seven. Seth inherits Grandstone Mansion and arrives to meet the servants. "Oh, no; I've no directions to give," said Seth, his dark handsome features breaking into a friendly smile. "I leave all that to you." He paused and grimaced, as if in sudden pain. "Is everything–?" began Pritchett, the gnarled old butler but Seth waved him away. "Lots of strong soup ... in two words," he explained. Then stepped sideways into a pastel-coloured bedroom where Rita, a raunchy blonde, lay on the bed, painting her nails. Later, he emerged, mopping his brow. Adjusted his belt, continued. Continued. "Steady! Here's somebody else ... Hullo! Here are more of them coming upstairs. There! there! All capital characters, and you shall all stop here along with me. What was I saying just now? Something about wine; so it was ... It's a poor heart ... a garden? Which side? I'll go alone, yes." With these words Splint descended the terrace steps in front of the house, crooning the 10th Psalm for thirty seconds or so then breaking off to whistle cheerfully a snatch of the theme tune from *L'Année dernière a Marienbad* as he opened an ornamental gate which led into a shrubbery, then sauntered along a winding pathway, both hands in his pockets. Ahead of him he saw the broad expanse of a flower-garden, flooded bright by the morning sun. On one side, an archway, broken through a wall, led into a fruit-garden. Apples, pears, that sort of thing. On the other, a terrace of turf led to ground on a lower level, laid out as an Italian garden. Wandered on, nothing human visible or audible. Seth ceased whistling. Removing from his pocket a pistol manufactured in Birmingham, he shot himself in the right temple, his last thought of the second helping of pears and cream which his mother had denied him on his seventh birthday. No. No good. Not interested. Only interested in getting back to sleep. In the little deaths, the big one waiting. In the tides of turning time. In that long ride to the airport. What long ride? What airport, where? Oh shut it. For God's sake. Call it "Off By Heart"? No. Clashes with "Paper Heart". One heart's enough. "Blue speedwell"? "The Wastes"? Or simply stick with the document title: *Offstory*. Meaning *off by heart*. Off by heart the lightning flashes, the steaming road, the driver with his gouged cheeks. The Hotel California. The Memory Motel. Oh come to the whitethorn that grows in the lane! Blue speedwell, pearls on primrose, the wastes ... Oh, shut it. For Christ's sake. For her sake. For my sake. For your sake. For God's sake. God? Don't make me laugh! No knowing, no. No knowing what happened, what might have happened, no going back. Stuck here, the bed, the keyboard, the low whirr of the hard disc. The rain, the cracked ice. A few more years left yet before 2007, eh? No need to panic yet. I am making my plans. I have not mentioned this to anyone but inspired both by H. G. Wells and the film *Explorers* I have been constructing a spacecraft in the backyard. Do not presume that I am ignorant of modern particle physics or the electroweak theory. All I require is one last trip to my local Homebase store and one or two minor adjustments and I shall then be in a position to attain ignition and head for The Cup, an ancient constellation representing the goblet of Apollo and which, according to the latest astronomical findings, "contains no objects of particular interest."

Got to get away, yes. Reaching the stage of misreading things. POWER TO SHIT DEEP DOWN STAINS. FAIRY EXCEL'S REVOLUTIONARY FORMULA EXCELS ON GREEKS. On November 8, 1984, a fine film of reddish dust coated the land for miles ...

Reaching the point where a speck on a wall scuttles away on a millipede's legs then dances back to its point of rest and becomes a speck again. A blob of pink toothpaste turning into a wireworm. Footfalls, fading, in the street. Silence.

Got to, yes. And should the spacecraft fail, the matter is not ended. Something more modest will suffice. One-hundred-and-sixteen easily assembled parts will do the trick. Collected from scrap metal dealers and junkyards, knocked up in a jiffy, do not underestimate me. I shall require a wide, quiet street for take-off but that can be arranged (diversion signs, cones, white and scarlet fencing, orange lamps filched from skips). Naturally I shall require a flat destination. From what I have seen of it in adventure films North Africa is just the ticket. I shall need to take a thermos and a leather jacket. There is space for one book (*Terres des Hommes,* naturally). Distant slam of a car door. Silence. More footsteps, two people. Couple having an argument. *But I do love you. I do.* Silence. *Fuck off, leave me alone.* Footsteps, gone. Silence. What's that? What one-hundred-and-sixteen parts? Glad you asked. I was alluding to the airscrew, the propeller boss, the boss plate, the 12-Cylinder 450 horse-power Napier Lion engine, the airscrew reduction gear casing, the carburettor, the engine bearer, the nose cone, the leading fuselage strut, the radiator, the radiator shutters, the radiator shutter control rod, the streamlined water header tank, the header tank filler, the waterpipe linking the aforementioned Napier Lion engine and the header tank, the engine's exhaust pipe, the oil tank, the oil tank stay, the waterpipe linking the header tank and the radiator, the valve operating lever, the valve lever control rod, the rudder bar, the wireless receiver and transmitter , the undercarriage strut bolt, the Triplex windscreen, the instrument board, the aerial reel, the cockpit, the wireless remote-control, the joy-stick, the pilot's seat, the elevator control lever, the logbook and spares box, the control wires to the vertical rudder, the cockpit floor strut, the wireless aerial tube, the collision bulkhead, the aerial, the front undercarriage struts, the rubber shock-absorbers with oil dampers, the landing wheels, the tyres, the wheel discs, the petrol tank fillers, the petrol tanks, the saloon curtains (may be dispensed with if of an extrovert disposition or with exhibitionist tendencies), the starboard windows, the leading edge of the upper plane, the starboard upper wing tip, the starboard upper plane, the starboard upper aileron, the registration letters (false, naturally), the inlet for the cabin's heating and ventilation system, the upper port plane, the upper port aileron, the aileron pylons, the aileron control wires, the upper port wing tip, a saloon containing up to eight wicker armchairs (should one wish to take along a party of Trotskyists for enlivening anecdotes and rigorous argument), the pilot tube of the air-speed indicator, the twin flying wires, the incidence wires, the streamlined hollow interplane struts, the port lower plane, the strut sockets, the leading edge of the lower plane, the fabric wing covering treated with waterproof dope, the solid compression rib, the rib flange, the former ribs, the main front spar, the ordinary ribs with holes in the web to make them lighter, the rib web without lightening holes, the internal bracing wires, the distance piece, the lower port wing tip, the main rear spar, the lower port aileron, the aileron gap wires, the trailing edge of the lower plane, the emergency exit hatch, the interior electric light, the life-belt, the roof light, the upper port longeron, the compact lavatory, the spare seat, the folding accommodation ladder, the port lower longeron, the fuselage side struts, the duralumin longeron strut sockets, the bulkhead, the fairing ribs, the fairing, the rudder control cables, the twin control cables to the elevators, the wire turnbuckle, the plywood covering for the fuselage, the fuselage bottom cross struts, the fuselage bottom bracing wires, the elevator control cross shaft, the port elevator control lever, the rudder cable guide rod, the elevator control rod, the fuselage side bracing wires, the rubber shock absorbers for the tail skid, the tail skid itself, the tail skid steel shoe, the tail plane, the tail plane trimming gear, the fin, the balanced portion of the rudder, the balanced rudder itself, the identification letter showing the craft's country of origin, the port elevator and last (but not least) the aerial plummet. A piece of cake. Now let me rest. Give dust a tongue or give me sleep. Distant slam of a car door. Silence. More footsteps, two people. Couple having an argument. *But I do love you. I do.* Silence. *Fuck off, leave me alone.* Footsteps, gone. Silence. And still wide awake, very. The surge rushing in, adrift. An empty beach, sand. Grey dunes. The old shipwreck far out. Rusted iron scraps lodged in the undisturbed sand. And no real sleep. The place of ferns and the place of rocks, the place of fire. Bredon Hill, so bitter cold. The

grass gemmed with dew. Leaves silver. Cracked ice on the
dented lid of the blue heart-shaped sand tray. The black VW,
the blazing headlights. Switch them off, yes. Can't get back, not
now. Too late, her fur coat, her long flowery dress. The wastes
of shining stars. Switch them off, off, off.

Off.

One Morning Twenty-Nine Carp Were Caught

1

Sitting on a swivel chair, at 3.50 pm on a warm afternoon in August, listening to Green on Red. Strange to think that Lenin never heard "Funny How Time Slips Away" (*strange that Lenin should have died*, said his wife; *I wasn't expecting it*).

"I just had a letter from Marx," Lenin wrote on September 8, 1900. A confidence to quicken the pulse and stir the mud of my ignorance and ripen the wild empurpled fruits of fancy. Oh, I see. Of course not. Not that Marx.

There is a famous photograph of Lenin and Leo Nikolaevich Tolstoy. They are on the balcony of Tolstoy's house. Tolstoy is sat on a high-backed cane chair at a table which bears a coffee pot and two cups. Tolstoy stares directly at Lenin; Lenin's gaze is focussed on the shadows beneath the table. Lenin's hands are clumsily heaped on his lap; he looks uncomfortable. There is a fly on Tolstoy's right kneecap, perhaps. Perhaps a tear in the cloth, with some pale, flaky skin showing and some white hairs. Or is it that curious table, supported by a single stout leg?

Gorki offered to send Lenin a gun. Lenin declined. "At one time I liked hunting, but now I am indifferent to it," he explained. Lenin said that he liked all animals except cats. For cats he felt only revulsion and fear.

Lenin's mother's father was a cloth merchant in Morshansk. He died of cholera during a business trip to Novocherkassk. His wife was away on a trip to the province of Vladimir – hence the name – when she received the terrible news. At once she hired a carriage and went off to visit the grave. She travelled across desolate plains and through dark, oppressive forests. She stayed at lonely, run-down inns, wedging table and chairs against the door at night. Some nights she even slept out in the open, under a rosy gorgeous sky, among garrulous crickets and the spasmodic screeches of neurotic, solitary birds. Who? Not that I recall, madam. No, sorry.

"When in doubt a writer should increase the difficulty," Lenin wrote.

The grave was never located and the widow settled, randomly, like gently falling dust, in bleak, creaky Taganrog, a small port of the Sea of Azov, her daughter Yevgenia, after the usual sequence of slippery events, giving birth to Lenin on January 17, 1860.

Five years earlier (hurry over this trifle, petty-bourgeois imperialist biographers!) Taganrog had been shelled by British and French warships. Thirty years before that Tsar Alexander I had died there, suddenly, for no obvious reason, though credulous serfs and pot-brained bourgeois insisted that the death was a sham, that the coffin contained another man's corpse, and that the Tsar had adopted the pseudonym Fyodor Kuzmich and gone off to Siberia, to live – and here all the birds of the forest begin squealing and squawking and defecating uncontrollably – a pure and holy life.

Lenin and champagne. On July 2, 1904, Lenin had difficulty breathing. Earlier, he had told his wife a comic story about some fat Englishmen and Americans. Uhh-ooh-aagh, gasped Lenin. Aagh-oogh. Oooh. Agh. They were going to send for oxygen but Lenin said he'd prefer a bottle of champagne.

Lenin's wife was called Olga. He wrote: "You are a little crocodile who has crawled into my heart!"

The idiocy of provincial seaport life. Lenin complained that Taganrog contained sixty thousand inhabitants who "busy themselves with eating, drinking, procreating, but no newspapers and no books."

In 1887 Lenin encountered a police officer who growled like a dog.

Four years earlier – *where's that champagne?* – G. V. Plekhanov wrote the first major Russian Marxist text, *Socialism and the Political Struggle.*

At Ragozina Balka Lenin stayed on a farm with a large Cossack family. The Cossacks killed bees, sparrows, swallows, magpies and ravens. At night, Lenin wrote, "my hosts fire rifles at some animal that is damaging the economy".

Plekhanov was the first Russian to argue that the working class was to play the chief role in the impending Russian revolution against the Tsarist autocracy. But the long years of exile isolated Plekhanov from changing conditions in Russia. He became increasingly out of touch with the mood of the labouring masses.

Lenin complained that on the train to Serpukhov people were only interested in discussing the price of flour.

Enter Chekhov, a revolutionist. Vera Zasulich told Chekhov that Plekhanov was a hound. "He will shake a thing for a while, and then drop it; whereas you are a bulldog – yours is the death-grip." Chekhov was pleased by the metaphor. "A death-grip," he repeated, with obvious delight.

In 1901, returning to Yalta after a short holiday in Italy, Lenin sent a telegram to Olga. *Health good. In love. Miss my dog.* Lenin often called Olga his dog.

Understanding Chekhov. On May 20, 1887, Chekhov's older brother Alexander was hanged. A plot to kill the Tsar.

1888. The Lenin family spent the summer on the estate of the Lintvaryov family. One of the daughters was blind, epileptic and dying of a brain tumour.

Lenin and trousers. As a child Lenin took lessons in tailoring. He loved disguises, dressing-up and practical jokes. He once made a pair of trousers for his second brother.

When Lenin was twenty-eight he decided to raise money to found a "climatic station" for writers. It would liberate them from politics and arguments. Nothing came of this.

Lenin and death. All his life he was attracted by cemeteries. After Lenin's death his friends were horrified when the coffin arrived in a dirty green goods wagon labelled FOR OYSTERS.

He read some of his stories to the dying Lintvaryov girl. She laughed. Lenin wrote: "What seems strange to me is not that she is about to die, but that we do not feel our own death and write as though we would never die." ·

At Lenin's funeral in Moscow the mourners got mixed up with the mourners at the funeral of General Keller of

Manchuria. A military band played slow, solemn music. Part of the small crowd mourning for Lenin solemnly followed the much larger procession for General Keller.

Lenin's return to Taganrog in 1887. He suffered from diarrhoea, the consequence of eating food prepared by his aunt. He drank heavily. He complained that the town was still plagued by dogs.

Lenin's weakness. Lenin had a weakness for uttering gnomic comments in an effort to stifle unwelcome conversation. Once, when everyone was excitedly debating Marxism, Lenin interrupted. "Everyone should visit a stud farm!" he said. "It is very interesting."

Lenin was also fond of Big Statements. On the disastrous first night of *The Seagull* he said, "Not if I live to be seven hundred will I write another play."

On another occasion he said: "There will be no revolution in Russia." Sipping the champagne, Lenin began to ramble.

2

It's clouded over. Green on Red move into "Don't Shine Your Light on Me". Restless, bored. The grey afternoons. The yellow afternoons. The black afternoons. The white afternoons. The afternoons of a lifetime.

On September 9, 1900, Lenin wrote that there was nothing new to report. It was hot. No rain. It was quiet, very nice, boring. It was much duller before Christmas than after; incomparably duller.

What solace?

Fishing.

Chopin. Beethoven.

In May 1885 the Lenin family went to stay at a house in Babkino, three versts from Voskresensk. Some days Lenin went fishing. One morning twenty-nine carp were caught. After dinner (8pm) everyone retired to the sitting room for drinks, conversation, whist, chess and music. Lenin particularly liked Chopin's *Nocturnes*. At the end of the evening the lights were extinguished and the governess played Beethoven's *Moonlight Sonata*. Lenin sat alone on the terrace, listening intently.

Lenin died in 1904.

Chekhov died twenty years later.

Nemirovich-Danchenko died nineteen years after Chekhov.

On 10 December, 1885, shortly after purchasing a new overcoat and a new pair of trousers, Lenin took the train for his first ever visit to St Petersburg.

Afternoons. Years. *Where's that champagne?*

On 26 April, 1893, Lenin complained of the "pain, itching, tension ... and such irritation throughout the entire body" resulting from his haemorrhoids. Four months and five days later, on 31 August, Anton Chekhov arrived for the first time in St Petersburg.

In the months and years that followed Chekhov wrote agitational leaflets and pamphlets, including *Explanation of the Law on Fines Imposed on Factory Workers* and *The Working Man and Woman of the Thornton Factory*.

1894. Lenin complained of a cough, palpitations of the heart and haemorrhoids. He wrote that he was weary of theories. *Once you philosophize,* he grumbled, *your brain starts whirling.*

While Lenin was bleeding from his anus, Chekhov met a young woman named Nadezhda Konstantinovna Krupskaya. "A story without a woman," chuckled Lenin, "is like an engine without steam."

Champagne, at last. Empties the glass slowly.

Lies down on his left side.

Stops breathing. Dies.

For three nights a week for five years (1891-96) Krupskaya taught workers in the industrial suburbs arithmetic, history and Russian literature.

In Yalta, Lenin denounced the local people as "utterly dull, drab and dismal."

Krupskaya remembered that *Anton Chekhov was interested in the minutest detail describing the conditions and life of the workers. Taking the features separately he endeavoured to grasp the life of the worker as a whole – he tried to find what one could seize upon in order better to approach the worker with revolutionary propaganda.*

"Proletarian! My poor brother! Honest toiler, exploited by the rich!" Lenin began a letter to his brother Alexander. His little joke.

1895. Chekhov was one of the founder members of the St Petersburg League of Struggle for the Emancipation of the Working Class. Its main activity was the issuing of factory leaflets. On 10 November Chekhov issued a mimeographed proclamation to the workers at the Thornton Factory. Meanwhile a spontaneous strike broke out at the Leferm tobacco factory and the shoe factory Skorokhod. December: Chekhov and five other members of the League were arrested.

Adolf Marx was a publisher. He offered to buy the copyrights of all Lenin's work for thirty thousand roubles. Lenin pushed Marx up to seventy-five thousand and excluded his plays. "I have become a Marxist for the rest of my life," he quipped. *Where's that champagne?*

In May 1896 the first mass strike in Russian history took place. It was triggered when textile workers in St Petersburg came out in protest against the non-payment of wages for the three-day holiday celebrating the coronation of Nikolai II. Soon it developed into a struggle for higher wages and a 10½-hour working day. *The strike spread to twenty of the biggest factories in Russia, employing 30,000 workers.*

"When I am 95, I will be getting a fearful mess of money," chuckled Lenin, 39, who had five more years to live. His friends advised Lenin against the deal and said that if he signed the contract he would regret it. He soon did. Year after year Marx made a fortune at Lenin's expense.

For the first time in the long history of the revolutionary movement in Russia, the revolutionaries had drawn the masses into action.

"I do find life a bore," Lenin wrote (November 1st 1896). "I have a sensation of nothingness, past and present."

3

First day of December ... Warm and muggy. November's Siberian snow all gone now. Snowman's carrot nose and sprout eyes rotting in the garbage sack. Hitachi Bass Boost System playing "Born to Fight". Warm up the undrunk mug of coffee.

I Saw the New World Born lying on the desk as GOR move into "We Ain't Free".

In Siberia Chekhov came to the conclusion that what was needed was a national newspaper which would fuse local Marxist study circles into a national organisation. Workers' leaflets circulated from St Petersburg to Kranoyarsk, from the Caucasus to the Urals. "All that is now lacking is the unification of all this local work into the work of a single *party*. Enough of our amateurishness! We have attained sufficient maturity to go over to *common action*, to the elaboration of a common party programme, to the joint discussion of our party tactics and organisation."

Lenin's friend the novelist and playwright Vladimir Nemirovich-Danchenko grumbled that the two of them never seemed to have serious talks any more. Lenin shrugged. What did Nemirovich-Danchenko expect?

"We have no political interests," Lenin retorted. "We are stuck in our profession up to the ears and it has gradually isolated us from the outer world ... To put it briefly, don't blame yourself or me for our silence and the lack of seriousness and interest in our talks, put the blame on what the critics call 'the times' or the climate, or the vast expanses, on whatever you wish and let circumstances take their own fateful, inexorable course, while we put our hopes in a better future ..."

February 1898. Lenin suffering acute pain. The dentist a blundering oaf. Gripped Lenin's troublesome tooth with the silver pliers. Hideous splintering noise. Broke the tooth. Blood everywhere. Had to come back in a week. Did so. The blundering oaf did it again! Blood everywhere. Had to come back in a week before the idiot succeeded in wrenching out the final shards. Agony. Blood everywhere. Infectious periostitis set in in the upper jaw. "My countenance became distorted," Lenin wrote. "I crawled up the walls with the pain. I had a fever like typhus."

(1898-?) wrote Chekhov. Onset of the period of disunity, dissolution and vacillation. *But it was only the leaders who wandered about separately and drew back; the movement itself continued to grow, and it advanced with enormous strides.*

Adding: "When [this] period will come to an end and the fourth (now heralded by many portents) will begin we do not know. We are passing from the sphere of history to the sphere of the present and, partly, of the future."

In the fall of 1899 Lenin wrote two long stories, "The Lady with the Little Dog" and "In the Ravine", and sketched out a third, "The Bishop". The first story, written shortly after he had first met the actress Olga Knipper, is about a man who perceives that it is "only now, when his hair was beginning to turn grey, that he had fallen in love properly, in good earnest – for the first time in his life." It ends: "both of them knew very well that the end was still a long, long way away and that the most complicated and difficult part was only just beginning."

On 1st May, 1900, there was a general strike in Kharkov brought about by the intense agitation of the revolutionary socialist local committees. In this strike, political demands were made which, in a sense, made the strike a turning point in the development of the Russian working-class movement.

Thirty-eight years after Lenin's death – ain't it funny how time slips away? – in 1942, Nemirovich-Danchenko received a Stalin award for *Kremlin Chimes,* a play about Chekhov.

In Moscow, between 23 and 26 February, 1901, workers came on to the streets in tens of thousands and fought the Cossacks. Moscow for the first time saw barricades in the streets. In March, and then again in May, mass demonstrations took place in St Petersburg. There were riots in Tiflis in April. In May the military laid siege to strikers at the Obukhov munitions factory in the Vyborg district of St

Petersburg. Eight hundred workers were arrested, and many of them were sentenced to hard labour by a military court.

How Lenin hated Yalta! Or so he said. *The idleness, the stupid above-freezing winter, the utter lack of pretty women, the pig snouts on the esplanade – it can all fray and tarnish a man in no time. I'm tired; I feel winter has been dragging on for ten years.*

Next to his house at Yalta was a cemetery. In July 1900 Olga Knipper came to stay. She was fond of humming "Don't Tempt Me in Vain". Soon she was going to bed with Lenin. On 6 August, Olga had to return to Moscow. Throughout August and September Lenin was preoccupied with *Three Sisters*, finally completing it on 16 October. Olga wanted to see him in Moscow but Lenin confessed to Maxim Gorki that he didn't feel like leaving. *The work goes on so well and it is nice not to feel the itching in my rear end that I had all summer.*

Rumours circulated that Lenin was going to get married. He denied them. "It's not true. I'm going to Africa to visit the crocodiles."

In December, depressed at the thought of a winter in Yalta, Lenin travelled to Nice. Olga was broken-hearted. *I can't reconcile myself to our separation. Why did you leave when you belong here at my side? Not until yesterday as the train was pulling out and taking you away from me did I clearly understand that we were separating. I walked after the train for a long time as if unable to believe it, and then began to cry as I haven't cried in years.*

In Nice Lenin revised *Three Sisters,* complaining that the play had worn him out. By the end of the month he was bored with Nice and keen to be off. He would have liked to go to Algeria but the weather was bad and the sea rough, so he went to Italy instead. He toured Pisa, Florence and Rome. In Rome it snowed.

Lenin returned to Yalta.

On March 4 1901 outside Kazan Cathedral in Petersburg mounted Cossacks charged students protesting against new laws restricting academic freedom. Several dead, scores wounded.

On May 25, Lenin and Olga were married in a small church on the outskirts of Moscow. Once they were married, Olga insisted:

that Lenin change his underwear regularly;

that Lenin brush his clothes;

that Lenin shine his shoes;

that Lenin wash his hair regularly;

that Lenin have his hair cut regularly;

that Lenin eat at regular mealtimes;

that Lenin take laxatives.

Chekhov at this time had recently published "Where To Begin?" (*Iskra*, No. 4, May 1901), the germ of *What Is To Be Done?*

That winter, 1901-2, a general strike of more than 30,000 students took place. In November 1902 a railway strike took place in Rostov-on-Don. Workers came out in solidarity in all the city's factories. During the strikes, mass meetings took place, many addressed by revolutionary socialist speakers. In July 1903 a new wave of strikes broke out, spreading over the whole of the Ukraine and Transcaucasia. Political strikes broke out in Baku, Tiflis, Odessa, Nikolayev, Kiev, Elizavetgrad, Ekaterinoslav and Kerch, involving around a quarter of a million workers. During the years 1901-3 it was workers, rather than peasants, nobles or intellectuals, who became the main opponents of Tsarism.

1900-3. The *Iskra* period. The period of preparation for the Second Congress. The period of suitcases with double bottoms. Anton Chekhov was so overwrought that he developed a nervous illness known as "holy fire". The nerve terminals across his back and chest became inflamed. On the way to Geneva he seemed agitated and restless. On arriving in Switzerland he broke down completely and had to rest in bed for a fortnight.

The twenty-second session! Discussion of paragraph one of the draft statutes defining party membership! Chekhov proposed that Article 1 should define a party member as one "who recognises the party's programme and supports it by material means and by personal participation in one of the party organisations." Martov preferred that the definition should end "and by regular association under the direction of one of the party organisations". Chekhov did not want armchair revolutionaries. But the *Iskrists* were split and Chekhov's proposal was outvoted 28 to 23.

And now comrades ... The editorial board of *Iskra*. Chekhov moved an editorial board of three members: himself, Plekhanov and Martov. Chekhov won. This was the question which split the party into the Bolsheviks (majority) and the Mensheviks (minority). Chekhov did not expect the split with the Mensheviks to last long. Nor did it seem justified to break up the party over such a trifling issue.

But the weeks pass. Things begin to slide. Plekhanov changes his mind, invites Axelrod, Zasulich and Potresov to join the editorial board of *Iskra*. Chekhov resigns in disgust, writes (18 December 1903), "The only salvation is – a congress. Its watchword: the fight against disrupters." But it took Chekhov eighteen months, until May 1905, to manage to convene the Congress and set the seal on the split with the Mensheviks.

By which time Lenin was dying, was dying, was dead.

1904: morphine injections, heroin. Forgot to take his dressing gown on a trip to Berlin. "I drank some wonderful beer yesterday" (June 6th, 1904).

June 16th, 1904. Olga away in Switzerland, having her teeth fixed.

June 28th. So hot. A mistake, bringing one's winter suits. *I am stifling and am considering leaving here. But where to go?*

Lenin would like to visit Como. Lenin would very much like to take the steamer from Trieste to Odessa.

From Trieste, yes. I shall wear a light flannel suit. I daren't eat the butter here. Shortness of breath. Only one remedy. Not to move.

When Axelrod was asked how it was that one man, Chekhov, could be so effective and so dangerous, he replied *because*.

Because there is not another man who for twenty-four hours of the day is not taken up with the revolution, who has no other thoughts but thoughts of revolution, and who, even in his sleep, dreams of nothing but revolution.

Complete immobility, that's the thing.

And no butter.

The Henry James Seminar at My Lai

Questions have been raised about the Henry James seminar at My Lai. The criticism has even been levelled that the seminar lacked the well-formedness outcome which is the desirable consequence of any organisation seeking improvements in product quality and enhanced customer satisfaction. The company has therefore invited the application of recently developed knowledge elicitation techniques in order that any negative entrenched attitudes or beliefs among team participants may be reframed to a more positive orientation. Through the application of rapport development and the erasure of communication inflexibility high quality information can be elicited enabling team members to become aware of negative cross-functional impacts which may be introducing elements of dysfunction within the parameters of the organization's target of reduced operating costs, increased productivity and improved product.

Gentlemen, ladies, colleagues, let me begin with some of the core values embedded in the company's program which do not simply contribute to the perceptual empowerment of team members but which also permit the enabling of a functional evaluation of negative attitudes in relation to the outcome of the Henry James seminar at My Lai. Core value one: *good decision making requires accurate information*. Core value two: *the intention of all behaviour is positive*.

Common sense? Precisely. I ask you all therefore to remember these core values when contextualising modes of pacification and quality control procedures involved in a strategic environment. What we are scrutinising here is the question of client and customer satisfaction within a problematic rural development situation relating to New Life hamlets, specifically the alleged lack of a well-formedness outcome in relation to the Henry James seminar at My Lai (4), Quang Ngai Province, Republic of Vietnam, 16 March 1968.

Contextualisation will also be assisted by conceptualising the seminar's physical space parameters. These were: the width of one football field (American); the length of three football fields (American). However, allowances must be made for thick foliage, bamboo trees, banana trees and other vegetation.

What are the facts?

The seminar lasted four hours.

A keynote speech proposing that Henry James's fiction yokes the European sense of the objective limits of life with an American sense of its limitless conceivable possibilities was prematurely terminated by tracer fire and exploding grenades and rockets along the perimeters of the group. The seminar then broke up into smaller discussion groups, with the emphasis on narrative technique and James as a novelist of manners.

Some problems were experienced almost from the word go. For example, a seminar participant was seen running with a copy of *The Notebooks of Henry James* when he was killed with a round from an M79 grenade launcher. It seems likely that this was an honest mistake, the cover bearing a remarkable similarity to *The Ghostly Rental*.

Before being judgmental about what eventuated it is necessary to recall core value one: *good decision making requires accurate information. As* Captain Medina explained, any sporadic shootings which occurred after lunch on the date in question were not in his line of vision.

Other episodes have been well documented. Infantrymen Bergthold and Maples entered a hut and discovered a copy of *The Jolly Corner*, around which were grouped three children, a woman with a flesh wound in her side and an old man who had been shot in both legs. Bergthold aimed his .45 pistol and blew the top of the old man's head off (an instinctive reaction to doppelgänger fiction, he later explained). Almost at once an elderly woman came staggering down a path. She was still gripping the copy of *The Golden Bowl* which she had been reading when someone shot her with an M79 grenade. The grenade had torn into her stomach but had failed to explode.

84

Though in considerable pain she insisted on paying tribute to the astonishing inventiveness of the baroque imagery in the final chapters.

Two middle-aged farmers were brought out holding a sheet of notes on *Watch and Word*, Henry James's little known first novel. Infantryman Boyce said their conclusion that *Watch and Word* ended in "melodrama" made him "kinda mad". He stabbed one with his bayonet, killed him. The second one he shot in the neck and threw down a well, dropping an M26 grenade after him.

"Literary criticism can be a powerful thing," agreed infantryman Roschevitz as he shot three seminar participants in the head with an M16 "for not having anything new to say about the first paragraph of *The Ambassadors*".

"It can cut both ways," added infantryman Simpson, with a hearty chuckle. He fired at a woman with a baby from a distance of about 25 metres. Her right hand was almost completely severed from the wrist, obliging her to drop her selection of James's criticism. Instead of saying whether or not she agreed with James that Swinburne's *Essays and Studies* all too frequently lapse into flagrant levity and perversity of taste, she ran off. Someone yelled to kill her *and* the baby. This was no sooner done than Hutson and Wright came across a middle-aged woman climbing out of a tunnel. She started to quote James's remark that the perusal of a story by an author who knows what he is talking about "is one of the most elevating experiences within the reach of human mind" when they machine-gunned her. As Wright indignantly explained, this was more to do with James's low estimation of *Our Mutual Friend* than anything *personal*.

8am. Medina radioed that fifteen seminar participants had been removed from ongoing discussions.

8.30am. Medina reported that 84 seminar participants had been silenced. As he explained later, not a single one of them could say where Henry James had been on the day of the great London unemployment riots in 1886; the single word "Bournemouth" would have ensured prompt medical aid, evacuation and a three-semester Nixon scholarship coupon, redeemable at West Lawrence College of Bible Studies.

From a mud and clay building emerged a mature student. He started to say something about James's surprisingly haphazard use of parentheses and of square brackets in the manuscript of *The Notebooks* when infantryman Crosley shot him just below the left elbow, severing his arm. At this a woman wearing a white shirt and carrying a baby came out. Defiantly shouting, "Foreign words and phrases are sometimes underlined in the manuscript of *The Notebooks of Henry James* – and sometimes not!", she managed to drag the man back inside. Hutson and Wright went after her with a machine gun and put an end to her pedantry.

In a rice paddy at the far northwest corner of the seminar a young girl aged eleven or twelve lay, shot in the chest. "What I remember most about *The Wings of the Dove,*" she whispered, "isn't the plot or the characters but the wonderful delicacy with which so fragile a web of human entanglement has been constructed." Leonard Gonzalez tried to give the girl some water. When he walked away he heard a shot and saw that one of his colleagues had asserted the superior merits of *The Ambassadors*.

In a clearing a group of fifteen seminar participants were gathered – seven women, three teenage girls and five children (who the week before had been allowed to sit up late to watch Marion Brando in *The Nightcomers*). One of these children, which was being held by its mother, precociously asserted that *The Pupil* would make an even better movie, a comment that was altogether too much for someone! A bullet zapped its way across the clearing and blew out the back of the child's skull. "Personally," said one of the teenage girls, "I think the spookiest of any of James's supernatural tales is *Owen Wingrave*." It is not clear whether this exasperated Hutto, Torres or Roschevitz, but soon everyone was firing into the fourteen seminar participants who remained alive.

Precocity was quite a problem that day. Another seminar group consisted entirely of children aged about seven years.

They ran forward with hands outstretched, proudly holding identical paperback copies of *The Tragic Muse*. "One of James's underlying themes is connecting the story of public and political life with the story of art," the group leader explained. Further discussion was muted by a sustained spray of automatic fire.

In another clearing an even larger group of seminar participants had been gathered together. Lieutenant Galley came along. Galley had always agreed with Ford Madox Ford that *The Spoils of Poynton* is James's greatest novel. When he heard someone whisper that *The Golden Bowl* was a symphonic *tour de force* he flushed. Galley didn't know French but he guessed it was a compliment. If there was one thing Galley couldn't stand it was James's late style. Galley got Meadlo to help him and together they sprayed the seminar group until Galley was sure he had curtailed all possible future discussion of suspense and emotional excitement in Chapter XXXVI of that difficult text.

The troops pushed on through the seminar discussion area. Meadlo arrived with Grzesik and found Galley with ten other members of the platoon. They had rounded up some forty to fifty James enthusiasts, including babies (who were drooling with pleasure as they fondled brightly jacketed paperback copies of *The Awkward Age*). The seminar leader seemed to be a Buddhist monk in white robes with a goatee beard. The monk was shaking his head and waving a copy of *The Portrait of a Lady*. Just then a child aged about two crawled away from its mother, gurgling what sounded very much like "Emerson" (almost certainly alluding to James's 1887 review of James Elliot Cabot's *Memoir of Ralph Waldo Emerson*).

Galley picked the child up, threw it down and shot it.

Various negative entrenched attitudes or beliefs have emerged in connection with this action (mostly, it must be said, from personnel displaying a wilful disregard for the company's target of reduced operating costs, increased productivity and improved product). But as Galley himself explained afterwards, "On babies everyone's really hung up.

The little innocent babies! But babies grow up. If your son is forced into a Henry James seminar and totally paralysed by the lack of narrative pace in *The Golden Bowl* you'll cry at me, 'Why didn't you kill those babies that day?'"

The monk with his copy of *The Portrait of a Lady* wasn't making any sense. Galley had had it up to here with these participants. "Load your machine gun and shoot these people," Galley ordered.

The entire seminar group was shredded by M16s. There was one final cry of *It is astonishing how one's wayside is strewn with ENDS after one has reached middle life!* – then silence.

The 2nd Platoon was particularly hard on seminar participants who were exploring the art-life problem in *Roderick Hudson*. One woman had a rifle barrel forced up her vagina and the trigger was pulled. One girl aged about seventeen was taken into a hut and raped by Hutto, Hutson and a third soldier (apparently she'd described the characterisation of Mary Garland as "weak"). When they were finished the girl's face was shot off. Several troops stood and watched, remarking on the timeless truth of James's observation that there are occasions when just to watch something can provide "an education of the taste, an enlargement of one's knowledge". Another young woman said *Roderick Hudson* had a serenity of tone markedly superior to James's other representations of Americans in Italy. For this she was sodomized by three platoon members, then raped by eight more, by which time others had heard of what was going on and came along to join in. When they were done they cut out her tongue, then mutilated her vagina with a bayonet. Regrettably some personnel with negative entrenched attitudes have commented adversely on such episodes, failing to contextualise them within cross-functional team methodology while at the same time overlooking core value two: *the intention of all behaviour is positive.* Additionally, there are many extenuating circumstances. Many of the girls and women who were forcibly buggered provoked their attackers by wearing silky black pajamas. Even senior officers, understandably, were unable to restrain themselves. As for Captain Kotouc, F2 intelligence officer, it was perfectly reasonable that he should be acquitted of assaulting and maiming a seminar member by cutting off the little finger of his right hand. Kotouc explained that the fellow was thumbing through *Washington Square* at speed, a look of insolence on his jaundiced face, offensively oblivious to the comic brilliance which informs every page.

I repeat, the criticism has been levelled that the seminar lacked the well-formedness outcome which is the desirable consequence of any organisation seeking improvements in product quality and enhanced customer satisfaction. In all some five hundred seminar participants died, and many others were injured, and this, in so far as it affected customer satisfaction targets, must be a matter for some regret. Additionally, while incurring no extra costs, the seminar discussion area was, undeniably, left in a state of disarray. It is important, however, to identify modelling processes in the complex world of experience and relate them to the company's overall goals. In evaluating procedures adopted on 16 March 1968 negative or obsolete belief systems may require re-framing or pattern-interruption in the context of the broader goal of American values and lifestyle programs.

It must be emphasized that the seminar outcome enjoyed senior management approval. Senior management had, and continues to have, every confidence in personnel who made interventions at the seminar. Benchmarking continues to be done into the successful marketing techniques involved in obtaining positive changes in employee satisfaction in relation to the seminar outcome. General Westmoreland himself sent a cable: CONGRATULATIONS ON THE OPERATION FOR TASK FORCE BARKER TO OFFICERS AND MEN OF C-1-2 FOR OUTSTANDING CRITICAL ACTION. The Pacific edition of *Stars and Stripes* ran a story headlined US TROOPS PUT REDS STRAIGHT ON COMPETING ABSOLUTISMS IN 'THE BOSTONIANS', CONFUTE 128. The *New York Times* ran a wire item about the mission's success. What's more, the prestigious *Henry James Review* carried a two-thousand word report entitled, "A New Approach to Henry James: Theme of Morality and the Self Undergoes Vigorous Interrogation in Quang Ngai Province Seminar".

Sadly, time is running out. There will be no opportunity for questions, nor is there any space left to discuss the seminar's contributions towards an improved understanding of *The Beast in the Jungle*, *The American* or *The Liar*. But the company is confident that Henry James himself would not have condemned any communications difficulties which may be conceded to have occurred at My Lai. "LIFE" he once wrote (with rare emphasis) "is less criminal, less obnoxious, less objectionable, less crude, more *bon enfant*, more mixed and casual," than the ridiculous concoctions of modern fiction – had he been reading Sharp, one wonders? – "and even in its most offensive manifestations, more *pardonable*."

And there you have it. Americans abroad mean well, but are liable, on occasion, to blunder. As Henry James knew, all too often they are deceived by wily foreigners. Medina, for example, was widely regarded as a warm-hearted man. Everyone testified to the warmth of his personality. Character witnesses for Medina included such fine soldiers as Brigadier General Lipscomb, Colonel Luper, Colonel Blackledge, Major Calhoun and *Washington Square* specialist Captain Kotouc. The company is confident that Medina was as committed to its overall goals and to the bringing of well-being, peace, comfort, confidence and success as anyone. Let no one forget what that other Henry – Henry Ford – once said. *Excellence in action means thinking laterally, progressing strategically and succeeding impressively.*

What conclusions can be drawn from all this? Point of view, as James himself well understood, is all important. It is all too easy to make snap judgments from the comfort of an armchair many years later. For the man on the ground, up to his neck in a confused situation and faced by possibly hostile Jamesians babbling of symbolic imagery and transcendent humanism, things are not so simple. As Captain Medina explained, how can you be sure that the fellow next to you is seeing the same as you? Has the other soldier turned his head away at the crucial moment, was his view blocked? What if the safety catch is off and a seminar member is several metres ahead of you or several metres behind, holding a copy of *The Princess Casamassima* in a suspicious or provocative manner?

In short, why is there all this fuss about the Henry James seminar at My Lai and so little about what happened during the Hawthorne seminar over at My Khe (4)? Why dig up the past when there are much livelier, more interesting things happening today, like the ongoing Iris Murdoch seminar in East Timor?

The thing to do, as all responsible and successful business people know, is to concentrate on the task in hand. Stronger institutional links between industry, finance and government must be forged to overcome tendencies towards short-termism. Investment in human resources is the precondition of competitiveness. Above all else, the thing to remember is that in any successful organisation seeking to improve work activities and enhance employee satisfaction within a framework of total quality control and increased productivity, strong feelings are best avoided.

Scenes from the 39-Day Strike at Thrabb's

Thrabb's Precision Gulliver Bolts

What we disliked about Thrabb's. Apart from the wage cut that triggered the strike. The banality and danger involved in the manufacture of Precision Gulliver Bolts under the capitalist relations of production prevailing at Thrabb's. Secondly: the Thrabb family. Flash Eddie and "Jiffy" Jools Thrabb, the sons of deceased Mr Harvey Thrabb, one of a long line going all the way back via James and George and Charles and Herbert and Colin and Frederick Thrabb (and others) to Andrew Thrabb, who, back in 1687, founded the Thrabb fortune with some fancy legal work which snatched away the wealth of a foolish, rich old woman who put too much faith in lawyers and found herself unexpectedly deprived of the five merk land of Kipplerig, the five pound land of Easter Knockward, with all the towers, fortalices, manor-places, houses, biggings, yards, orchards, tofts, crofts, mills, woods, fishings, mosses, muirs, meadows, commonties, pasturages, coals, coal-heughs, tenants, tenantries, services of free tenants, annexes, connexes, dependencies, parts, pendicles, and pertinents of the same whatsoever, a fortune which, shifted to Yorkshire and manufacturing, provoked the famous "Thrabb Ultimatum" of July 1812, which asserted *that Charles Thrabb has been guilty of diverse, fraudulent and oppressive acts – whereby he has reduced to poverty and misery 700 of our beloved brethren and has obtained the sum of £15,000, actuated by the most diabolical motives, and therefore we, the General Agitators, do adjudge the said £15,000 to be forfeited and do hereby command Thrabb to disburse the said sum, in equal shares among the workmen,* which Thrabb responded to by calling in the militia, killing two, injuring thirteen, all part of that glorious year 1812 when there were 12,000 troops stationed in the north of England to repress the working population (more than Wellington had under his command at this time in the

Peninsular Wars). All the same, the Thrabbs. Charles's son, George a notorious skinflint, exploiter, drunkard, liar and cheat, qualities which earned him a marble tablet in the local church (*Never in Drink, nor told a Lye in all his Life, & most Honest in all things*). Harvey Thrabb, like his predecessors, built up the business through years of hard tax avoidance work, dishonesty, fiddles, wangles, donations to the Conservative Party, foreign holidays and other services granted to the officers of the local Council, donations to the Police Benevolent Fund, foreign holidays with the Chief Constable (who bore an uncanny physical resemblance to the fat, dead swindler and one-time Home Secretary Reginald Maudling), agreeable police dinners, sweeteners, cases of whisky to the Director of Planning, massive exploitation of working people over sixty years, Thrabb instinctively grasping the essentials of Marxism – the extraction of surplus value, the drive to capital accumulation – even if the rat-moustached officials of the local branch of the Union of Associated Grinders & Grunge-Worples didn't, wanting no truck with left-wing extremism or/and nonsense of that sort, we-live-in-a-democracy-Gawd-bless-Her-Majesty-jest-you-wait-'til-we-get-a-Labour-Government-my-lad. The foreman, death's head face, emaciated, Joe Lobb, lackey, creep and crawler, hated trades unions, adored the Royal Family, read *The Daily Express* of course, stern surveillance of anyone who spent more than thirty-five seconds over their bodily functions, tugged at his forelock so often and so hard that one day he pulled out a bloody, dripping chunk of his scalp, causing witnesses to allude to those sticky and crimson scenes where the cyborg's human disguise begins to wear away in *The Terminator*.

before day one
The thump and crash of machinery, headaches, fatigue, every day a fog of monotony, pistons, whirring blades, the crash of plates, the pumping of pumps, the interaction of circuits, the pressing of buttons, the presence of wires and broken mesh, you can hardly think straight, fuddled and fatigued, you're in a stupor, a grey zombie, but there's also a sullen rage, a waiting.

day one

Immense elation. The vote overwhelming. We rushed outside, talking excitedly, formed a crowd by the gates. We walked to and fro, blocked the entrance. We walked and talked and by the end of that day had exceeded our daily average quota of 18,000 steps, Derek managing 27,025. Then the police arrived. Inspector Ferret. Pointed features, eyes like slits, yellowy complexion as if jaundiced. Sergeant Manganese, big, red-faced, the constipated, sour expression of a man who hadn't defecated for nineteen years, four months and twenty-nine days, and could feel his wastes inside him, layer upon black iron layer, like a bullion warehouse. PC Dullard, bovine, moustached, lumbering, big-booted. WPC Shallow, blonde and shrill, squawking, hostile, ripe for promotion at Belsen, orders is the thing, obey orders. PC Acne, just out of Hendon, looking about thirteen years old, a slightly bewildered expression on his pink-yellow face.

day two

"Get back over there!" snarled Chief Inspector Prickett. "Otherwise I shall arrest everyone under Section 57 of the Repression Act, 1994, for conspiring to bring about an irruption of alexandrine verses of twelve syllables."

day three

From the left pocket of his gaberdine jacket Dave produced a comb, from his right pocket emerged a square of wrinkled white paper. Combining the two Dave produced a meltingly beautiful rendition of Wagner's Siegfried Idyll, a performance marred only by Harry's fart. Iris said if she was ever stranded on a desert island with eight musical recordings she would want one of them to be Rachmaninov's Sacred Concerto "Mother of God in Never Slumbering Prayer" by the Joyful Company of Singers. Doris lit a cigarillo, causing an explosion. To everyone's considerable surprise Harry shot upwards into the air and vanished from sight, in the general direction of Uranus, discovered on March 13, 1781, by William Herschel, in

Bath, the greenish colour of which owes much to the high proportion of methane found in its atmosphere.

day four
"Whether lameness and halting do still increase among the inhabitants of Rovigno in Istria, I know not," confessed Culpepper.

day five
"The sky is dark as polished whale-bone!" cried Sue, who had spent a fortnight in Iceland.

day six
"I see that stock markets around the world went into free-fall yesterday with more than £12 billion wiped off share prices in London," said Jane. "Yes," said Fred. "The London market lost 2 per cent of its value. The FTSE index plunged 63 points to 3085.6." "It's a crying shame," whispered Doris. "By the way, what exactly *is* the FTSE index?" "It measures Britain's top 100 companies," Ron explained. "I've never really understood how the stock market works," Jane interjected. A sheep trotted past in the distance, followed by seven others. They seemed nervous. "All I know is that share prices have been depressed by falls in the prices of bonds," Alan said. "Bonds are government debt," he added. "Markets are falling because other markets are falling," said Iris. "Shares have fallen because bonds have. It's no more than that," concluded Dick. "Just look at those sheep!" cried Ray. "I've never seen blue sheep before." "Me neither," said Len. "It probably means there's an Italian film director in the area," Steve added. "Or an inexplicable localised downfall of blue liquid of a substance which, when analysed, will prove to be unknown to science," asserted Sue, a keen reader of the works of Charles Fort. "Or something to do with a defective airliner," said Charles, a sceptic. "Or some sort of stunt filmed for a party political broadcast," speculated Jill. But none of us were prepared for the pink-and-green striped baby elephant which lumbered

briefly into view by the semi-erect gasometer, then turned and galloped towards Sheffield with surprising agility.

day seven
A discussion of doppelgängerism as a symptom of alienation under capitalism.

day eight
The discussion continued, ending at 4.45 pm.

day nine
"Did you see on the news last night that Sierra Leone's population has a life expectancy of 38 years, and out of 1000 children born, 200 die before their first birthday?" asked Jane. Everyone shook their heads; they'd seen the dolphin/the football match/the royal tour. "That's because it wasn't on," explained Jane.

day ten
Ray was humming "Democracy", one of the better tracks on *The Future*, Iris reckoned (though the album as a whole wasn't a patch on *I'm Your Man*, said Dick), which provoked Ron into a monologue on both the song and the subject. "The song breaks down at the point where the singer says he's neither Left nor Right ... It turns into an anthem for the bloody Liberals. Democracy! By which all anyone ever means is bourgeois parliamentary democracy or one-person-one-vote in a form as atomised as possible so that the isolated individual can be as influenced as much as possible not by solidarity and fellow-feeling and discussion but by the numbing "common sense" of the mass media, a fog where strike days are "lost" and trades-unionism is of little interest unless it can generate the street theatre of "picket line violence". Democracy! Characterised by its sheer bloody *infrequency.* Eight to ten minutes in a lifetime. Pathetic. Jesus. No wonder the Chartists called for annual parliaments. And what sort of democracy? Democracy by piddling *geography*! And have you ever been round the

palace of Westminster with an MP? I went round once with a new Labour MP. Nye Goddotson, remember him? Everywhere we went there were these flunkeys looking like penguins, bowing and grovelling and "Good morning Mr Goddotson, *sir*." It really was just like how you'd expect a fucking palace to be! You couldn't help but feel physically dwarfed by the architecture. Huge rooms with fifty-foot-high ceilings, endless wood-panelled corridors, walls loaded down with dark turgid paintings. And the MPs are made to feel so fucking *important*. The only bit I really enjoyed was where you got to see Charles I's death warrant. And the chambers! Ludicrous places. The Tories putting down prayer cards to reserve their places on the benches, evil hypocritical arseholes. And the voting lobbies! Totally bizarre. A couple of desks on rails pulled out so that the MPs have to filter out between them. Cretinous. As Lenin so lucidly pointed out, parliamentary democracy 'always remains, and under capitalism is bound to remain, restricted, truncated, false and hypocritical, a paradise for the rich and a snare and deception for the exploited, for the poor … deceit, violence, corruption, mendacity, hypocrisy and oppression of the poor is hidden beneath the civilised, polished and perfumed exterior of modern bourgeois democracy.' Now if Cohen could only write a song putting forward *these* perceptions …" Ron gave a sigh and relapsed into silence, chewing satsuma segments.

day eleven

A crisp frosty sparkling October morning, pure blue sky, sun blazing down. The morning of the book discussion at the factory gates. Mary said she loved Fay Weldon. Mick said you couldn't beat a good Jack Higgins. June said she always read a few lines of Georg Trakl before going to sleep. John recommended *Pseudodoxia Epidemica* by Sir Thomas Browne. Iris said she loved Ruth Rendell. Tom said John Berryman cut to the heart of things. Dick disagreed. Dick said for his money Marx's *Economic and Philosophical Manuscripts of 1844* still had a lot going for them. Steve urged everyone to read Stephen King's *The Shining* ("and, at all costs, avoid the film"). Helen asked if anyone had read *Finnegans Wake* (only June and Iris had; June liked the ending, Iris said she'd found it a bit slow). Rob put in a word for *El Libra de Los Seres Imaginarios* (the word being "eumorphous" – though for a knotted, dizzying two minutes and thirty-nine seconds – two minutes and thirty-nine seconds of a curious molten thrilling that spread and spread 'til he was carried away with the last, blind flush of extremity – he had considered, in prickly, lustful turn, "estiferous", "estuous" and "euneirophrenia"); Rod said no one should reach fifty without having read *The Voyage of the Beagle* at least twice, commending the book for its invaluable explication of *all the waters here have puna* and *where there is snow there is puna*, expressions which, though commonly encountered in the Cordillera, might well prove perplexing to passing tourists; Ron, inaudible as always, applauded June, and muttered (the mutterings pieced together at a later date by redeployed members of the West Midlands Regional Crime Squad) that he could only bear narrative linearity if it involved a structure of oscillation (yes) which superimposed itself (I done it, I confess) on a vectorial line (give me a pen, yes) disseminating contingency (yes) and multiplying signs (guilty, guilty, guilty), lacking the final determinations of a closed structure and loosening events and plot to the point of (regrettably the papers in this case are no longer available) disappearance. At which point a bus came round the corner bearing scabs and we all ran into the road, shaking fists and bellowing SCAB! SCAB! SCAB!

day twelve
"Those who despair of a mass fightback are missing what is really going on!" cried Doodle, surging forward. "People are changing because the system makes them change!" agreed Harry, visibly turning from watery pink to a lively blood-red. "Some people are already hitting back!" said Polly, interposing herself between the factory gates and a five-axled juggernaut bearing important freight. "More are ready to do so if given a lead!" whispered John, who was wearing a yellow T-shirt bearing the words EAT MORE CUSTARD.

day thirteen

A grey dawn, grey as despair, with a chill drizzle which thickened into a light, persistent rain. Iris stood by the factory gates looking glum. "Cheer up," said Dick. "It may never happen." He chuckled a manly, hairy-armed chuckle. "Triste la lluvia," whispered Iris, shaking her head. "Que sobre el mármol cae, triste ser tierra. Triste no ser los días del hombre, el sueño, el alba." Dick frowned. "Hey, Fred, what's the little lady saying?" Fred deftly applied forefinger and thumb, the thumb still a little flat from the long years of thumbsucking, and squeezed the rain from his moustache. "Little lady she say ah-you ignorant sexist pig," he said, in a Mexican-Glaswegian accent. Then he slapped Dick on the back and laughed. "No, seriously comrade, what Iris is saying is that this fine sleet has feelings, that the rain feels mortified, even inconsolable, and as it falls and vanishes is undergoing soul-searching, evoking in its translucent shallows qualms and melancholy, pangs and regrets – *maladie du pays*, as it were as it falls, falls, falls down upon the marble and drips into the earth, quite spent, full, now, of futile regrets and watery longings, a sad rain, sad to be no longer part of *us* on the picket line, of humanity, sad to be leaving behind the dreams and the dreaming and the struggle for a better, unimaginable world where capitalism will not exist, where Thrabb's Precision Gulliver Bolts will no longer exist, sad, in short, to be no longer a part of this astonishing morning, in this drear suburban street." "What marble?" said Dick, in a possibly ironic voice. "I don't see no marble." "The marble of things that are hard and pitiless," whispered Iris; "the marble of privilege and palaces; the marble of monuments and fallen Tsars; the marble of death and graveyards and curious angels with primitive harps and drugged faces." "I'm with you now," said Dick, grinning. He wandered away humming "I Wish It Would Rain" and was shortly afterwards arrested for threatening behaviour.

day fourteen

Reg held a quiz. The prize was a copy of Miliband's *Capitalist*

Democracy in Britain. The two questions were: (i) on whose estate were the most grouse shot in Britain on a single day?; (ii) how many grouse were shot? John guessed it was the Duke of Westminster's, but no one knew the number. Reg gave us four possible answers: (i) 804; (ii) 2,921; (iii) 693; (iv) 1056. Everyone guessed, correctly, that the answer was 2,921. Vicky mentioned the curious disappearance of two species of protected birds which eat grouse, the hen harrier and the peregrine falcon, from the Duke's lands. Two lorries were turned back. The day concluded with an interesting discussion of what should be done with the Duke of Westminster, the Duke of York and the Duke of Edinburgh.

day fifteen
"Ideas do not come from thin air!" yelled Polly at five-past ten, synthesizing Shakespeare and Marx. "You what?" said blond Fred. "Ideas are rooted in the material conditions of life," replied Polly. "She means we live in a corrupt, competitive capitalist world scarred by exploitation, racism and sexism," chipped in Reg. "Yes," said Polly, who had been born in Newcastle and who had a brother in Southampton.

day sixteen
Not much happened on day sixteen.

day seventeen
The day Ron explained the meaning of *Blow-Up*. He said the film was really a subliminal evocation of the still unsolved mystery of the JFK assassination. He babbled of picket fencing, monochrome foliage, dapplings of shadow, lurking figures, the need for better enlargements. Polly asked if anyone had noticed that Zapruder was actually standing to the rear of the fence where the second gunman was commonly believed to have been standing, a fact evident only in rare showings of the complete footage. Ron became agitated and was led away for an ice cream.

day eighteen

On day eighteen a plump beaming saffron-robed Buddhist who greatly resembled the Buddha dropped by and urged everyone to abandon the strike. "Give up this folly, my friends! Retreat and practise the six yogas of Naropa as taught by the venerable Lama Yeshe. Give up meat, alcohol, garlic, sex, television, music and tobacco! Calm your mental chaos. Recognise that the greatest obstacle is expectation! Pray at 4 am. Meditate for 49 days in total darkness. You'll feel much better for it!" "Fuck off, sport," retorted Dick, who had Australian blood in him and was seriously fond of imported lager. It was only when Dick tore the robe from the Buddhist that we discovered it was Eddie Thrabb, wearing a mask.

day nineteen

"Okay, so Chinese Communism sucks," said Dick. "No doubt about it. Mao was a Stalinist arsehole. The Chinese invasion of Tibet was an obscenity. Having said that, what gets up my nose is the way all these fucking middle-class pseudo-Buddhists go on about pre-invasion Tibet as if it was some kind of workers fucking metaphysical paradise. In fact it was a miserably poor country where the population was fucking *shrinking* thanks to VD and mass starvation. The people were serfs ruled over by a vile and murderous feudal ruling class. The place stank of oppression and death. All that's happened over there is that one foul regime has been replaced by another one." Erica, an anxious expression on her face, steered the conversation away from politics, brightly enquiring if anyone had heard Terry Evans's *blues for thought* album. But no one had.

day twenty

"Not many people seem to know of the Japanese medical profession's hostility to the Pill," said Dick. "Abortion is for many Japanese women the usual method of birth control. Interestingly (in the light of the events of two days ago), Buddhism plays an important part in this disgusting state of affairs. The cult of Jizô identifies aborted foetuses as *mizuko* or 'water children' which may be floated away while permitting the possibility of rebirth with the conception of a new child who is, literally, the aborted child reborn. As Crump says, what is interesting about all this is that it demonstrates how two major institutions of modern Japan, the medical profession and the Buddhist clergy, both dominated by men, combine to deny women control over their own sexuality, and so drive them into a state of trauma, for which one side then provides physical and the other emotional relief, making a vast profit in the process."

day twenty-one
"Obscene in their self-consecration," bellowed Dick – he was alluding to the Government's privatisation programme – "the kings of mine and rail and soil can find no better occupation than living on our blood and toil!" He broke off to explain that Jane was unavoidably absent, away shooting periscopes. The highlight of day nineteen was the turning away of five lorryloads of pig-iron and a discussion of Magritte's "Le survivant", which in turn led on to an animated debate about armed struggle, Ireland, Stalinism, Latin America, and the perplexing absence of newspaper, TV or radio reportage of the blue sheep and striped baby elephant.

day twenty-two
The day Derek denounced the erotic life of modern man. "The erotic life of modern man is doomed from the start!" he yelled, ignoring Penny's titter. "It is doomed because the quest for the beloved is hopeless, hopeless, hopeless. It is this very hopelessness which breeds the maggots of disenchantment, the worms of cynicism, the cancer of self-hatred. It is doomed because modern copulation is doomed. Our fucking is filled with guilt! Our caresses are frayed and burning! Love is doomed because sex has become the aspirin for our foul frustrations and sickly, yellowish defeats! Copulation has become an anodyne for the sticky, sluggish soul-sickness which oozes out of inner corruption! Our orgasms have become the

shuddery outlet for angry and destructive feelings which besmirch the name of love! Love is doomed because our quest for erotic fulfilment is joyless and sterile. Inescapable is man's restlessness! Eternal is the frustration which is the inescapable condition of our erotic life!" "You speak for yourself, love," said Polly. Dave explained in a whisper that Derek had developed some rum ideas ever since he'd started devouring the novels of D. H. Lawrence. "Personally I blame *The Portable Nietzsche* which he got for his birthday. I warned Mike it was bound to lead to trouble but he just wouldn't listen."

day twenty-three
"The Egyptian mummies that I have seen," remarked Morris, "have had their mouths open, and somewhat gaping." Ted asked Morris if he'd ever been in a post-modernist story and Morris said not to his knowledge, no.

days twenty-four to twenty-eight
It rained. Forty-seven arrests were made. Fifteen for "Behaviour Likely to Lead to a Breach of the Peace" (on the grounds that the act of picketing Thrabb's Precision Gulliver Bolts was thought likely to provoke Eddie Thrabb into breaching the peace). Eleven for "Obstructing a Police Officer in the Execution of his Duty" (a police officer is executing her/his duty if s/he is preventing the occurrence of a socialist act). Four for "Obstruction of a Public Highway" and preventing the passage of three ants and a beetle. One for "Criminal Damage" (the dent in Eddie Thrabb's Buddhist mask). Six for "Disorderly Conduct" (i.e. behaviour that causes harassment, alarm or distress to a capitalist). Ten for "Non-Capitulation" (i.e. an action or actions indicating a refusal to accept a reduction in wages or conditions of service, an offence under the "Capitulation of the Workers Act, 1996").

day twenty-nine
One of the comrades began humming "Mr Tambourine Man", unwittingly instigating the day of the Bob Dylan discussion.

Ron said he'd been amazed to discover the song was written in New Orleans in February 1964. He winked and said anyone who'd seen *JFK* would know what he meant. Everyone looked blank, and Ron explained that Dylan might well have passed David Ferrie in the street. He might have sat next to him in a bar. Who? You know, that guy who was mixed up in the conspiracy. Gerry interrupted to say that the problem with Dylan was he'd gone from writing hard-hitting songs like "The Lonesome Death of Hattie Carroll" to garbage like "Joey". A fierce debate about Dylan's best and worst albums broke out. A consensus was arrived at that *Slow Train Coming* was very definitely the worst, but no one could agree on the best. Harry said that though the lyrics were ideologically unsound nothing haunted him quite so much as the Bootleg Series version of "Every Grain of Sand". Someone wondered why Dylan had never become a revolutionary socialist. Nick said he supposed it was because Bob had never met the right girl. Just then a thunderstorm exploded overhead and everyone ran for shelter.

days thirty to thirty-seven
It rained. Fifty-four more arrests were made for exactly the same offences as listed on days twenty-four to twenty-eight.

day thirty-eight
"Ordinary people can become giants when they move against the system which wrecks their lives!" said Harry, passing round the bacon sandwiches. Doris nodded. "I feel six inches taller since I came out on strike," she observed. "Six weeks ago I would never have been interested in the diversity of socio-economic forms and epochs, still less perceived that classical political economy was a system of thought which suppressed and denied the historicity of economic relationships and in-stitutions, eternalizing the particular patterns of capitalism as perennial traits of civil society as such." "Me likewise," said Al.

day thirty-nine |
The Union's national office reached an agreement with the

Company. Everyone would take a 10% pay cut and agree to work an extra twelve hours each week for no extra cash. Under this agreement everyone would be taken on again, except for twelve known troublemakers and people with green eyes. The area official of the Union said it was the best deal that could be reached in the circumstances. Fifty-one per cent of the strikers voted in favour, forty-nine per cent against.

day forty
Ron stands beside Rita outside the factory gates, his green eyes shimmering. "It is only a matter of inches!" he cries. The breeze snatches the rest of the sentence and drags it away. Black hyphens whirl anarchically past the archaic crimson telephone box on the corner, making Dick think of Keats and Sterne. Harry slyly picks at the patch of dry, flaking skin on his left elbow. The sky begins to darken in the west, the darkness releasing curious expanses of livid yellow and garish amber. In the old hut, Polly puts the kettle on. In the circumstances there is little else to do, other than to prepare for the afternoon seminar on Serge. Iris continues lovingly to model her wax doll of the area convenor. Jack sits on a stool reading Thomas McGrath's "Letter to an imaginary friend". Jill drops by with the pins. The absence of mass pickets, the little makeshift shelter, the beginning rain: it would be easy to feel depressed, easy to feel like packing it all in and emigrating to Miranda, Ariel, Umbriel, Titania, Oberon or some other moon, but she doesn't, she isn't depressed, no, what she feels instead is a glow, the after-glow of struggle, a drift of warmth which pushes away the chill of extinguished possibilities. One day ... One day there will be another struggle, one which will ignite a hundred other struggles, a thousand, ten thousand, a hundred thousand, catching fire, boiling and bursting out, fusing, toppling the old structures, a thought evoking that moment in *Dr Zhivago* when the major stands on the water-barrel to harangue the deserters, and the lid gives way ... The little makeshift shelter, how redundant it seems now. Soon it will be taken down, thrown away. But not yet; not today. Today it is

unexpectedly poetic; today it speaks of something momentous which has taken place and left behind a residue. The words to speak of this seem stale and over-used, grey slogans mouthed by dilettantes. Jill goes inside to speak to Iris. Outside, Arthur is still inflating the General Secretary. Garth whistles "It's All Over Now, Baby Blue" with a surprising jauntiness, while, as usual, shaking his raw pink fist at the sky and at all the surrounding capitalism, grizzled Albert begins once more to quote from irrepressible-and-relevant-as-always Marx.

Claremont

Down, down, into darkness, the lens cap, the black plastic lens cap that goes spinning away, bounces once on the black bars of the gutter, then falls back, slips neatly between, down, down into the darkness, amid the bobbing shadows, unnoticed by the buoyant protesters, a trivial tiny occurrence on a bright sunny July day. Bright bright day, yes, so long ago it seems now, history, a sunny July day in 1993, standing on a wall not far from the Orient ground, waiting for the march to pass (and *click* – here they come), far more people than you'd expected, a long procession coming across the valley, from Hackney, entering the Borough, passing sunlit along Ruckholt Road, York Road, Maud Road, Station Road, up the steps at the end, crossing Langthorne, down more steps into Colville, snaking briefly on to Grove Green Road, then turning right, into Claremont Road, London Ell, dark leafy trees, dense foliage, summer's shadows, then scarlet wallflowers, bright window-boxes, signs in windows, defiance, all vanished now, gone in the dreams, the shadowland, the darks, as dreaming again of Claremont I dream of the tower, much bigger than it was, wider, scores of protesters standing on the crossbars, and wake, wake to the memory of rubble in the rain, the remains of the tower dumped, tilted, on a rubble pile, the entire street bulldozed, no wish to linger here, no desire to stay by the thick grins of the guards, the stupid ignorant historical faces, get away from them, take three quick shots and get back on the bike, pedal back up Grove Green Road in the drizzle, demolition lorries everywhere, up Fillebrook, almost all of the houses there gone now too, fallen like playing-card houses, a smear of mud and rubble wiped through the neighbourhood, impossible ever to come here again without the gigantic memory of it, the bender site that last morning, drifting away at eleven, returning at two to find it all over, the chainsaw whining, branches crashing down, the shocked weeping girl, arm-in-a-sling, the dumb lines of hard-eyed police, traffic passing, an ordinary miserable grey afternoon, the sort of ordinary miserable grey afternoon in which State murders, gross injustices, are committed, you didn't stay to watch any more, cycled away, it was over, an experience of defeat yet a victory of sorts, Twyford desecrated (but Oxleas saved), the link road built (but not yet the Newbury by-pass), and reading *The Experience of Defeat*. Going back now and then (the cold, the graves, the army of police), going back to that cold semi-derelict house, rear windows barricaded with silver sheets of corrugated iron, pinpricks of light, the roaring that went on all night, and as you lean out of the window the lens cap slips off the camera, off the ledge, plummets into the floodlit dirt below, lies there until the next sweep of the street by the dirty yellow bulldozer, gone now, buried, the sudden memory of how this has happened once before, the year before, that very first day you got involved, that very first No M11 Link Road march, down and down it went, abruptly, into darkness, the lens cap, the black lens cap spinning away, bounces once on the bars of the gutter, then falls back, slips neatly between, down into the darkness, on a bright sunny long-ago July day, when you walked towards Claremont, not knowing where it would lead, a long procession coming from Hackney, along Ruckholt Road, York Road, Maud Road, passing along Station Road (where the lens cap slipped through your fingers), up steps, down steps, along Colville, turning right into Claremont, leafy trees, scarlet wallflowers, bright window-boxes, signs in windows, snapdragons.

We searched for Sharp but he was nowhere to be seen. We tried to see the trees, the houses, the rainswept Green but all we saw was a monotony of traffic. We stared at the hollow, rotted trunk of the old chestnut tree on George Green. It was scorched at both ends where someone had tried to burn it. We stared at the place on the Green where the trunk of the old chestnut tree used to be rooted. We stared at the cranes and piledrivers and orange pipes. We stared at the sunken road, the passing traffic. Impossible to imagine how it was before for those who were not there. We searched for traces of Sharp and Claremont. We stood beside a concrete wall, by the speeding cars and lorries. We stood, drenched in fumes, feeling estranged. The mood upon us was a sour, grey one. We departed the neighbourhood in low spirits. Some stories end bleakly, with the street inimical, scraps of paper blowing around, dead walls.

We left East London. It was only later, climbing Golden Cap, that the mood shifted. The sandy crest was luminous with Hollywood sunlight. A blue-winged moth skipped hither and thither about the bushes. From the summit we stared down at dormant Charmouth, misty Lyme, the foam-flecked bay. Shafts of shifting sunlight played across the dappled fields from restless, boiling clouds. The great bay glinted with shots and shards of grey metallic light.

Since You Went Away

Absurdity, this! This, yes! Everything! Fortunately almost done. Almost done. Clean shaven and not far now. Foot down hard, skimming the ruts. Talk of *Thelma and Louise*! The empty talk, the feathery inconsequential words. Trivia on a breeze. And all the big unmentioned things. Swinging the wheel from side to side, *The Blue Danube* booming, everybody laughing, having one hell of a good time. Ah, this breathless starlit air! Ah, the dizzying abysses! Ah, how all things hang like a drop of dew upon a blade of grass! This what? This society. Fool Nellcock quoting Shelley, of all asterisking things! What a bleeping joke! This idle trade. Almost done. What a relief! To all and sundry; to all concerned. With what strift and pains I bring forward these backward things. Asking. Sober questions. From the dead and deep part of the night. In E17. Almost done. Almost complete. Done in. As complete as incomplete can be. Torn between Trotsky and the butterflies. In emotional arrears. Depleted. In reach of the sea, drawn to the recess. Adieu! Adieu the heart-expanding bowl! Athwart. Azure. And round thy phantom flesh glue my clasping limbs. A long, dead calm of fix'd repose. Absent I follow thro' th' extended Dream. And now begin to live at the old rate.

Zeds and zero. The zero line. The zeal of fools. Zee end. As in: *Once, at a sunlit gas station in Washington State*. Once, at a sunlit gas station in Washington State, he remained in the car, watching as she crossed the forecourt to pay. A red setter dozed on the warm concrete by the kiosk. She went over and patted it. While she was paying, he observed a chunk of snow as big as a man crack free and sluggishly slide down the corrugated roof. It smashed softly in a broken heap behind her. She didn't hear it or notice it, paid for the gas, came back. "Okay?" she said. Okay. And they drove on.

Resolved by the Parliament, That the Book entituled, A fiery flying Roll, Ec. composed by one Coppe, doth contain in it many horrid Blasphemies, and damnable and detestable Opinions, to be abhorred by all good and godly people.

Distorting days. Die Veneris, 1 Februarii, 1649. The day burns like an oven. Distorting days. The day, that day, the day after, the following days. The day after day after day. The dead days. The days, the days. Dread has followed longing, my darling. My darling and dearest. I am speaking of dying and death and the dead. Disdain? Dispute my heart. Dim lights of life that burn a length of years.

Goes without saying, it. Gone, gone, gone to dust. As Greensleeves' arse. The vast blue flashings of the rotating light on the patrol car. A desperate gulph! G is for the gates. G is for the grasshopper longing to leap. G is for the girl with the electric c—. Or the goblin. Who now the fool alarms.

Too often has it happened that, when history has taken a sharp turn, even progressive parties have for some time been unable to adapt themselves to the new situation and have repeated slogans which had formerly been correct but had now lost all meaning – lost it as "suddenly" as the sharp turn in history was "sudden".

Bucket. A broken bucket. Bucket-seat. Bucketing down with rain. Bob. Bob Dylan. Buckets of rain. Beauty. Beauty, beauty, beauty. How? O no there's none. Breasts. Breasts flat and fallen. Breasts swelled and corrugated. Wrinkled. Begin the preparation. The bygones, let them be. Old Baudelaire. The burning questions. Burning letters. Breach of the peace, Dr Bones! So stamp out those smoulderings. Today the bucket will draw no water. Tuck into the beans and bacon. Because. Because of the Increasing Night. Bedridden. But yet to be right myrie wol I fonde. Like a bit of stone beneath a broken tree.

Quarter after one in the morning. A hot sticky day slips into a hot thick sleepless quartered night. Quartered by the quart of vodka times, the ice, the green broken glass in an alley, her quivering green green eyes. Quarter after one in the morning like in *Le Salaire de la Peur*. The Qliphoth. I'm clean-shaven and a hundred years old. A thousand. Quavery. I'm quit of all that (all what?). Questions. Queer questions. Absurdity. Tied.

Meatloaf singing "It Just Won't Quit". Quibbles. Quiddities. And quickly turn away.

Ordered by the Parliament, That the Book entituled, A fiery flying Roll, Ec. composed by one Coppe, and all the printed Copies thereof, be burnt by the hand of the Hangman, at the New Pallace-Yard at Westminster, the Exchange, in Cheap-side, and at the Market-place in Southwark.

Xanthochroic? A life of xerophagy? X is for xeroxed cheeks and kisses on cards and letters. X is for sufferers from xero-phthalmia and xerostomia, who shudder at the sight of xysters.

What's that? Will you, won't you? What's happening? With a fa, la, la. A tale like the wandering moon. W is for Wenatchee. W is for when and where. When self is swept away and gone. When all those rooms and passages are gone. Where the nettles bunch. Saplings root among the broken stone. Westering clouds, hurl, speeding.

E is for the end of *A Sentimental Journey*. E is for empty bed and early worms. E is for ebb-water and Eve's custom-house. E is for eccho (the old spelling). And end, ends, endings and extremities.

Every particular slogan must be deduced from the totality of specific features of a definite political situation. And the political situation in Russia now, after July 4, differs radically from the situation between February 27 and July 4.

Troubles, business, voyages. Twenty years! In a trice, gone. Time upon a once. And every year carries something with it, away. The tintamarre ended. Now cold like you, unmov'd, and silent grown. Time's filthy load. Ended? Tumultuous thauts. The return. The return to Dover, broken. Hubbub of a Sealink ferry, shouting teenagers, voluble aunts, grey opaque windows, a dismal grey-green sea, screens booming a documentary, guardsmen, castles, the Queen, Shakespeare. To Victoria in a carriage crammed with Germans. "These are my family," beamed the corpulent, friendly father to the ticket collector, who grunted, crashing the door behind him. Kent in the rain, the parochial suffocating dead awfulness of England. Back to the room in N3. The room was dead, stripped of your presence.

A vault for a dead one. Since you went away I have heard Elvis Costello singing "After the Fall", Loudon Wainwright singing "The Picture". T is for Twyford Down and Group 4 and the Southern Area Intelligence Unit. T is for texts and time. Time upon a once. The texts? Try Sir Thomas Browne, *A Letter to a Friend*. Try *Lord Jim*. *East Coker*. *To the Lighthouse*. As for the time. It was 17.09, like in *Gunfight at the O.K. Corral*. Frankie Laine was singing along. I said, "It's just the way the cards fall." I said, "It's too late for both of us." And you said: "Okay, doc." (No, you didn't.) Twenty years! Like Heathcliff I have had time enough to reckon my groans. Let me die when the moon is in motion from the meridian. Take me from this tumult, this noise, this quivering, this restlessness, this boredom. The unjust unmentioned things. All that planetary suffering. And then? Ther is namoore to telle.

Virelay. Voiceless, where the voices and footsteps are dead. Void of all desire. No, not quite. But getting there. Stupefied in a poise of inaction. Void of all design. Returning to my narrow selves. And the last last house of all.

Fol de rol, fol de rol. Festivities recede. The FIN exploding out of the monochrome screen. F is for a frugal life. From the apparent What conclude the Why? Festivities recede, yes. So what's left? Frailties, flames. Faded eyes. A puckering of the upper lip. Flinders. Fatalities, names. Faithful to its fires, this heart – Funerals of former fucking seasons. Thou cruel Fair, I go. Through minutes, years, and days, and hours. For ever, then, farewell.

Ordered by the Parliament, That the Lord Major and Sheriffs of London and Middlesex, be enjoyned and required to take care that the same be done in the places aforesaid within their respective Liberties; And that the Bailey of Southwark by enjoyned and required to take care the same be done in Southwark accordingly.

Hours. My choicest hours. The hours of tenderness, gone. Haply I – Heart's purple. Hang your heart upon ... Harrowed in Harrogate. Handy- dandy. The hurly burly. Hopeless lasting flames. When it's done. Hide it, my heart. Hope, despair, resentment, regrets. *Haec olim meminisse juvabit.* One day it will be useful to remember all this. Your hairy sprindge.

Intact! Just about. I'll no more play at chuck-farthing. If there's not too much sun nor too much cloud. In the quiet sanctuary of a simple room with clean linen in a green valley in a nation at peace he clung to her. Until inexorable Death shall level all.

Join griefs to thy griefs. Jot it down while you can, why not? It's all a joke.

We said that the fundamental issue of revolution is the issue of power. We must add that it is revolutions that show us at every step how the question of WHERE actual power lies is obscured, and reveal the divergence between formal and real power. That is one of the chief characteristics of every revolutionary period.

Kidney vetch? Kedgy and keen in Kentish Town. Kistvaen, konixope, kymograph, kapnography, katabolism. Kisses. Kecks. Knells. Kelpie, Kirsten. Kelp, kells and kegs. Kerbs! And kidney vetch. *Kyrie eleison.*

Lat go, farewel! L is for what lost Niamh murmured. L is for longing. My dirty leaves, leave them now. Last pangs. Life's idle business at one gasp over. Last sparkle. Lop, lopped, long-gone lust. A long leave I take. *Ordered by the Parliament, That the Sergeant at Arms do forthwith cause diligent search to be made in all places, where any of the said Blasphemous Books, entituled, A fiery flying Roll, Ec. composed by one Coppe, are or may be suspected to be, and to seize them, and cause the same to be burnt at the places appointed; And that all persons who have any of the said Books in their custody, do cause the same to be burnt at the places aforesaid.*

Maundering here, and maundering there. Maudlin and miserable. Meditating M—'s merkin. Mulling things over. München. Münchausen. Mulligrubs. The murage. The escape into books, movies. Movies? Since you went away I have seen dozens. Scores. Hundreds. I have seen – "Oh but it's your watch, you shouldn't just leave it!" – *Since You Went Away.* I have seen (again!) *Jaws* and *Brief Encounter* and *The*

Romantic Englishwoman and *The Man Who Fell to Earth* (but I have not been back to *The Man Who Would Be King* or *Voyage to the Centre of the Earth* or *Robin and Marian*). The murage. Masks. Mirth and Opium, Ratafie and Tears. The daily anodyne, the daily analgesic. Monorhymes. To kill time and thought. Mute the tuneful tongue. You did well, Mordaunt. Metaphrasts. And the mountain throws a shadow.

N is for news and names. Or news of names. What name, what names? What's the news? That name awakes all my woes. Hush, now. Silence. Say none, then. Speak of noons and nights. The old usual things. Hot nights, cool noons. No. No more go a-roving. His nibs. Nothing, no. Never, never, never. The name of this game is Solitaire. Now it's ended. Now say no more. Say never. Never to have looked into the eye of day. All that story finished. And another begins.

All agitational work among the people must be reorganised so as to make clear that it is absolutely hopeless to expect the peasants to obtain land as long as the power of the military clique has not been overthrown, and as long as the Socialist-Revolutionary and Menshevik parties have not been exposed and deprived of the people's trust. That would be a very long and arduous process under the "normal" conditions of capitalist development, but both the war and economic disruption will tremendously accelerate it. These are "accelerators" that may make a month or even a week equal to a year.

Clear from the tumult, salt and dirt of tides. Communicating still, in Canterbury verse. Cup empty. Closing eyes, now. Darkness falling over the couch. Where I lay dull and muddy. The darkness falling. C is for Claremont. Curtains. Curtains dangling in a smashed window. The waste spaces, the bricked-up doors. When I was a child the candle setting light to the kitchen curtain. Christ knows what it was made of, lace? Went up WHOOF in a single vast unforgettable sheet of flame. The green curtains in that ground-floor cul-de-sac flat, we kept them closed. The green curtains of that little room overlooking the grass. From chair to chair. Crazed. Cup empty. Closing eyes, now. Cast your eyes upon paper. Consider these lines, these lies. Call me a dull sullen prisoner in the body's cage. Conceal. Concealment. Coming, another think. Command old words that long have slept to speak. The chaunt on my lips.

Ordered by the Parliament, That all Majors, Sheriffs and Justices of Peace in the several Counties, Cities and Towns within this Commonwealth, be required to seize all the said Books in all places where they shall be found, and cause the same to be forthwith burnt by the hand of the publique Hangman.

O is the great globe or the zero. O is the cry of lust, the death gasp. O is for once upon a time. Once, at a sunlit gas station in Washington State ... *Once, I remember* ... Since you went away these three words batter my heart. *Once, I remember* ... Since you went away these three words pummel me intolerably. Since you went away, only wisps and flinders. Once, I remember, at a sunlit filling station on the long road to Wenatchee ...

Under the warm sun's comfortable heat, you? Coldly I imagine. Warmly remember. Under you. Under the green cool sheets, the house on Larch Street. *Parfum exotique.*

Preposterous! Paltry time. Pangs. Pinions. The place where I us'd to sit fooling in private. And so the plaintive numbers flow.

The substitution of the abstract for the concrete is one of the greatest and most dangerous sins in a revolution.

Rag Fair take these spent pages. These remains. Repent old pleasures and solicit new? Resolution and a ball. The road I must walk when dead. *Rinasce il genio antico* ... R is for ruin. R is for Ronald. R is for Regicide. R is for *Rigoletto*. Ruins toured at a leisurely pace. Castles, abbeys, circles of erect stone. Carnac. Ruin, wreck, wrack, absurdity. Repeat no more that killing voice.

A new cycle is beginning, one that involves not the old classes, not the old parties, not the old Soviets, but classes, parties and Soviets rejuvenated in the fire of struggle, tempered, schooled and refashioned by the process of the struggle. We must look forward, not backward. We must operate not with the old, but with the new, post-July, class and party categories.

Spleen that for six days had seiz'd me. Sleep gone, now. Sound of a stick upon the floor. What day was that? Sunna, Mona, Tiw, Woden, Thuner, Friga, Saetern. A sonsy slut? And *sem to you.* Scrawls with desp'rate charcoal. Stanzes irreguliers. Sol through white curtains shot a timorous ray. Time snatching away the words, the words. The skein so bound us ghost to ghost. Since you went away I have done what I must. I have climbed fences, run through mud. Been chased and seized by men in yellow jackets bearing the word SECURITY. Why, only the other day two police officers warned me if I did not get down from the big green crane they would arrest me for breach of the peace ... Peace! Sleep gone, now. Since you went away I have never been able to forget the waterfall. *Die Wasserfall.* A milk-white fast foaming torrent gushing between dark narrow rock at the edge of a wall of dense pine forest, coldness, purity, seamed with racing bubbles, melted ice from the tongues of the great slabbed glaciers high away at the desolate beginnings of the great tributary valleys. Since you went away there have been days, there have been days. Skywriting, propellers droning over a Spanish beach. Clouds like lovers' bodies. Soft intercourse, soul to soul. Soft, soft. The melting residues.

Of course, in this new cycle there will be many and various stages, both before the complete victory of the counter-revolution and the complete defeat (without a struggle) of the Socialist-Revolutionaries and Mensheviks, and before a new upsurge of a new revolution. But it will only be possible to speak of this later, as each of these stages is reached.

Years following years. Something gone ev'ry day. You, your face, your skin, yes. A puckering of the upper lip. Lines. Year in, year out. At last they steal from us our selves away. Frolicks. Amusements. A girl, a woman, a friend. Leaving me with nothing, no. Nothing more to say. Here fynyssheth (Oh won't you kindly come with me, come with me, come with me, come

with me, come with me, come with me, come with me, come
with me, come with me, come with me, come with me, come
with me, come with me, come with me, come with me, come
with me, to the broken and bitter end) the boke.

Speech

Comrades, we have today heard many moving testimonies to the obscenity and injustice of the slave trade. Some may have been exaggerated, some irresponsibly simplistic, but I think that whatever differences we may have on this subject everyone here today agrees that slavery is an intolerable injury to human nature! *(Applause.)*

It is for this very reason, and no other, that emancipation must be approached with great circumspection. Conference has before it a motion calling for instant abolition of slavery and the slave trade. Yes, I hear you. Some of you may cheer. But it would not be honest of me if I did not remind you of our Party's greatest strength. In a word: *pragmatism*. In two words: *pragmatic realism*. I believe it was Shakespeare who said, "To hear the bells of victory ring, Pragmatic realism's the thing." Or to put it another way: abolish slavery overnight and what would be the result? I will tell you, in one, simple, chilling word: *anarchy*. Abolish slavery overnight and you have a recipe for anarchy. Get rid of the slaves and what then? I will tell you, comrades. *Chaos*.

I will tell you something else. I have not become leader of this great Party of ours to see a people – our people – their people – *any people* – plunged into anarchy! *(Applause.)* If I ask you to vote against this motion it is because we on the National Executive Committee care passionately about the slaves. And let me say something else. We are not afraid of resisting the easy option. We've all heard them, haven't we? "Abolish slavery," the abolitionists say, just like that. Many, I don't doubt, are sincere, though some, it must be said, are extremists. But have the abolitionists thought of the consequences? Have they ever considered the slaves? Have they ever thought that slaves will require a lengthy period of tutelage before they are able to exercise the responsibilities of freedom? A state of things in which the negro escaped the necessity for labour would be as bad for him as for his owner. He would be cut off from civilising impulses! He would have no incentive to better his condition or to impose any but the slightest degree of discipline on himself! He might well become a more degraded being than his ancestors in Africa! If I stand here before you today and oppose abolition it is for one reason and one reason only. It is because I have the best interests of the slaves themselves at heart! *(Tumultuous applause.)*

But though we have a responsibility to the slaves, we must not forget other responsibilities, chief of which is the responsibility to our own seamen! Yes – our very own sailors! The slave trade has been rightly described as the nursery of the British seaman. Let me ask you a very simple question: who would deprive a child of its nursery? Who would deprive our seamen – the finest seamen in the world, incidentally! *(enthusiastic applause)* – of training and experience? Are our competitors abolishing slavery? No, my friends, they are not! Are we to turn our sailors into a second-rate force of men simply to satisfy the prejudices of a group of do-gooders with a sentimental attachment to blacks? *Of course not.* Comrades, I have a plan – *A Business Plan for Britain. (Applause.)* It involves partnership! Challenge! Colonies! It is a plan to get Britain moving again! *(Applause.)*

My friends, it would be very nice to say: *tomorrow, slavery is abolished! Tomorrow, the slave trade is ended.* We would all feel very good, would we not? But we live in the real world, the world of give and take, of compromise, of civilised discussion. We are, are we not, pragmatic realists? I know it has been said before, but I shall say it again: *politics is the art of the possible.* Is abolition possible? My friends, I am certain that it is. But not today, not tomorrow. That is why the National Executive Committee recommends the setting-up of a committee of enquiry into these matters. The committee will meet on a regular basis, every two years, and will draw up a programme of action for abolition. It may not be possible to implement abolition during the lifetime of a Labour Government. There may be difficulties, problems, snags, complications, impediments, handicaps, obstacles, sticky wickets, ticklish situations, inconvenient circumstances, things that go against the grain and hinder, aggravate and make impossible. We shall have to wait and see. We are realists, not dreamers, and we are not ashamed to be realists! *(Applause.)* Until the committee of enquiry has deliberated the matter it would be improper of me – of anyone – to jump to rash conclusions. Comrades, that is why I am asking you to oppose this motion. For the sake of our seamen – for the sake of our nation – above all for the sake of the slaves themselves – I ask you to vote against the motion. Say NO to easy answers! Say NO to irresponsibility and chaos! Say NO to abolition! *(Thunderous applause lasting eight minutes; motion overwhelmingly defeated.)*

Cavell: Her Life in Vegetables

1. The Turnip

March 13, 1865. The Reverend Frederick Cavell, like most clergymen, was an avaricious bore who suffered from gas, bouts of impotence and an uninteresting variety of moderate, watery, religious delusions. He had married Miss Louisa Warming because she was a good plain little woman who could cook and sew, because she never disagreed with him and because she had enticing thighs he wanted to squeeze. Miss Warming was his housekeeper's daughter; she was ten years younger than Fred; she had no prospects; she naturally consented to his mumbled proposal of marriage. Before the marriage he arranged for her to go to a finishing school, in order to learn about cutlery, deportment and vegetables. Her potato soups were delicious. But there was still the problem of his impotence. On that cold blustery night in March 1865 nude Louisa lay, as usual, in an agreeably narcoleptic state, eyes tightly closed, broad thighs spread wide, and only the faintest of saltmarsh reeks to hint of hidden lubrication, and, as always, her flawless intimidating breasts resembled two perfectly formed puddings, concocted of ice and cream, while, with grim inevitability, the sight of her pubes reminded Fred of that sinister dried seaweed you saw clinging to the rocks at Pentire Point, so that, as ever, his penis refused to stir and thicken, pummel and coax it as he ever-so-desperately might, with gentlemanly discretion, beneath the crisp white cotton sheet. He had Shakespeare to thank for what happened next. While his fingers and thumb maintained their barren exercise his mind, idling through the years, abruptly fixed on the open-air performance of *As You Like It* he'd attended in Penge, on a sultry June night in 1859, in which the country girl Audrey had, for the sake of verisimilitude, strolled on to the stage sucking a turnip – no ordinary turnip, either, for as the

Programme had pointed out it "had been plucked near Anne Hathaway's cottage". Though almost everything else to do with the performance had long since crumbled from memory, he still vividly remembered sluttish Audrey and her pale, ithyphallic turnip, and suddenly, re-remembering, he was astonished to discover himself possessed of a massive, swaying erection – and so it was that on Monday, December 4, 1865, Edith Cavell was born.

2. The Courgette

Swardeston lay deep in the drowsy idiocy of rural life, in the same deanery as Humbleyard, not many miles from Norwich and Nowhere and not far from lacklustre Bracon Ash, monotonous Stratton Strawless and the awesome parochial banalities of Hethel and Little Snoring. Edith Cavell's early years were stupefyingly boring, numbed by knitting, jam-packed with jam-making, crammed with prayer, hogwashed by hymns, fat with phatic conversation and, worst of all, made turgid by the cretinous whackings and scurryings of lawn tennis. When Edith was eleven years old the maid, Brown, pencilled in capitals on the wall of her attic room: THE PAY IS SMALL, THE FOOD IS BAD, I WONDER WHY I DON'T GO MAD. Perhaps it was the moody, embryonic Bolshevik Brown who first lit the spark of rebellion in Edith, for it was not long afterwards that the Reverend Cavell went into his study and was appalled to find Edith insolently puffing on a cigarette. Worse was to follow. "The Choice of Valentines" was Edith's own discovery, in a leather-bound volume of Thomas Nashe her father owned but had never read. Exactly where Edith obtained the courgette from, however, is unclear. The fact remains that she was caught by her mother, knickers around her ankles and a dreamy expression on her rosy face, *in flagrante delicto* with a foreign vegetable. Edith was promptly despatched to austere, authoritarian boarding schools over a hundred miles away, at first in London and then Bristol. But it was no use. She had discovered the importance of vegetables, sex and rebellion, and her life would never be the same again.

3. Sprouts

In 1886 Edith went to work as a governess in Steeple Bumpstead, where she discovered the pleasures of sprouts which have only been very lightly boiled, gobbling plate after plate of them, topped with a knob of yellow butter. The deep, rich crunchy texture made chewing and eating almost as much of a sensual pleasure as defecation or masturbation, and she knew there was only one place in the world where she wanted to be: Brussels. In 1890 she became governess to the four children of a prominent advocate who lived at 154 avenue Louise. Experts have estimated that during her five years in Brussels Edith Cavell ate five hundred kilos of sprouts. She might have joyfully eaten another five hundred had it not been for that momentous meeting which occurred by the vegetable stall on the avenue de la Toison d'Or.

4. Onions

Rosa Luxemburg was born in Zamosc, a Polish version of Steeple Bumpstead, on 5 March, 1871. By 1895, like many young women of twenty-four, she was exhausted and dis-illusioned with life. Some days she did nothing but stay indoors, listening to Leonard Cohen records. It was at this time in her life that she went twenty-seven times to see *Nurse Anna Neagle*, a futuristic P. K. Dick movie. It portrayed a British woman in an imaginary Belgium colonised by sinister spiky aliens who wore goggles and said nothing but "zurr". Nurse Neagle smuggled Magritte prints to the Inverness Liberation Movement but was betrayed by the author of a monograph on Constable. In a much praised comic scene President Richard Nixon made a global television address, stating "The maintenance of order could never require the murder of a woman". Then the aliens secreted a toxic substance into Nixon's sweat glands and the President melted. Luckily Sharp, the priest who visited Neagle in her death-cell, was a disguised metafictionist. The words *It is God swill* caused the roof to fall in and the pair effected an escape by aerostat. Drifting over Chur, lack of oxygen made them wild with desire. Beneath dark, fleshy reflections upon the swaying glass the berserk compass needle was an unnoticed grey blur upon a silver disc. Ballooning over Everest, they crashed. Neagle died, impaled on the peak, her face bathed in celestial light. Her lover, smiling strangely, escaped on skis to the music of Tangerine Dream. Critics compared it to *Girl on a Motorcycle* and *The Spy Who Came in From the Cold*.

Rosa Luxemburg's melancholia deepened when a friend loaned her *The Trinity Session* by the Cowboy Junkies. She was also morbidly aware of her limp, the result of a hip disease in childhood. Then there was the suffocating climate of capitalism. As a teenager she had involved herself in revolutionary socialist politics. The times had seemed exciting ones, with strikes breaking out all over Poland, massive May Day demonstrations and everywhere the throb and pulse of socialist possibilities. But in 1889, tipped off that she was about to be arrested, she was obliged to flee from Poland, to become a political exile in Zürich. Here she fell in love with another exiled Polish revolutionary, Leo **Jogiches**. But how quarrelsome revolutionary socialists are! Jogiches fell out with the great Plekhanov! Rosa and Jogiches squabbled on questions of ideology with the leaders of the Polish Socialist Party (PPS)! They launched *The Workers' Cause* newspaper! Their faction split from the PPS and formed a new party, the Social Democracy of the Kingdom of Poland party!

By May 1895 Rosa Luxemburg had had enough. She was bored by Marxist economics; she was tired of Jogiches; she was sick of speeches and paper sales. She wanted something more out of life. She went away to Brussels for a few days for a rest and to think things over. And so it was that Rosa and

Edith, falling into conversation about the price of a kilo of onions, and then about other things, decided ("Oh, I wish I could be *you*"; "And I wish I could be *you*!"; "Well, what's to stop us?") to swap identities. Rosa Luxemburg departed for London, where she became an Assistant Nurse, Class II, at the Fountains Fever Hospital in Tooting, giving her height as five feet three and a half inches, and against the question, "Where educated?", writing: "Kensington". Edith, after a crash course in Polish, limping, Russian and the fundamentals of Marxism, went off to Zürich. The first time she climbed into bed with Leo Jogiches she was a little apprehensive that he might notice there was something *different* about his little sugar plum, but fortunately his mind was deep in organisational questions. In the first, prickly flush of excitement at discovering the joy of pseudonyms, Edith tried out another, publishing her first pamphlet as "Maciej Rozga". But it lacked the resonance of "Rosa Luxemburg". The pamphlet addressed the national question, and argued that the struggle for Polish independence was a diversion from the class struggle. Marxism, class struggle and economics, she realised, had turned out to be every bit as exciting as they had sounded! In the spring of 1897 Edith Cavell presented her thesis *The Industrial Development of Poland* to the University of Zürich, and became a Doctor of Law.

5. Tomatoes and Potatoes

On 20 May 1898 Edith Cavell moved to Berlin and shortly afterwards wrote one of her most important books, *Reform or Revolution*. It addressed the problem of poultry-yards, worn-out slippers, social reformist lemonade and the reactionary weighing of little piles of cinnamon and pepper. In short, it constituted a dazzling assault on the degeneration into parliamentarism and reformism of the revolutionary foundations of the German Social Democratic Party (SPD).

Her private life could have been happier. Jogiches, just like a man, kept making excuses. *If only you'd settle your citizen-ship, finish your doctorate, live with me openly in our own home. We will BOTH work and our life will be PERFECT!*

To leave Zürich after ten years without a doctorate – very unpleasant indeed. She remembered the old days, the happy days. She would always associate Jogiches with tomatoes. How often, how delightedly, had her little piglet spooned her delic-ious tomato soup! And those wonderful afternoons at Melide when Dyodyo sat on the porch, sweating, while she trudged down to the garden with her "Administrative Theory" notes! And the times he came back from Lugano regularly at 8.20 pm with the groceries! *Oh, Dyodyo, Dyodyo! Hurry up, come here; we'll hide from the whole world ...*

How about living in Hamburg? Out of the question! The weather reminded her too much of the Swardeston years. *The Hamburg climate is very harsh and foggy, similar to England's.* Instead she acquired a wonderful flat with courg-ette and tomato-coloured walls at 58 Cranachstrasse, as well as a cat named Mimi.

1905. Mass strikes and revolution in Russia! January lightning, spring and summer thunderstorms! Time for a new pseud-onym: "Anna Matschke", journalist. But she was caught and imprisoned. Her hair began to turn grey. She looked yellowish and very tired. Released, but there was worse to come. In 1907 she learned that Jogiches had involved himself with a Polish comrade named Izolska. The news reached her while she was peeling potatoes in her apartment on the Cranachstrasse. Konstantin Zetkin was there. Her shoulders trembled; she burst into tears. Konstantin put his arm around her. He was only twenty-two, and inexperienced with women. One of the potatoes bore a strange resemblance to a phallus. Laughing through her tears, Edith dragged him into the bedroom.

6. *Runner Beans*

29 July, 1914. Edith Cavell sits silent and withdrawn in the Cirque

Royal, Brussels. Strange to be back in that city, after so many years, so many speeches and meetings and pamphlets ... And now the world is on the brink of war. *The Bureau of the Socialist International is urging proletarians of all nations to intensify their demonstrations against war!* But the proletarians are overjoyed that there's going to be a war! They're waving their hats and bonnets in the air and cheering! And the SPD deputies vote for war credits! And Edith is arrested for agitating against the war and put in the women's prison in the Barnimstrasse.

Here, to fool her enemies, she adopted the pseudonym used to attack the ministry of the Duke of Grafton in the pages of the London *Public Advertiser* in 1769-1772 and published *The Crisis of German Social Democracy*, which refers to Japanese torpedoes, Prohaska in Ueskub, Putumayo, cannibals, a twelve-metres-high sculpture by F.A. Bartholdi, nutshells, Hungarian pigs and prunes, bacon, cocoa powder and coffee substitute, but which deliberately avoids all mention of vegetables in its blistering attack on the war and the socialist movement's abandonment of class struggle and internationalism. Tomatoes were never far from her mind, however, as is shown by her definition of imperialism as "the product of a particular stage of *ripeness* in the world development of capital".

The weeks turned into months, the months to years. She was released, then re-arrested. She remembered earlier, happier times, especially her cat, her kitchen, her lifelong interests. "Do you remember those runner beans I cooked after the French manner?" she wrote to Sonya Liebnecht on April 19, 1917, seven months before the November revolution in Russia, predicting that it would fail not because of Russian backwardness "but because Social Democracy in the highly developed West consists of miserable and wretched cowards who will look quietly on and let the Russians bleed to death". It is, she added, "an act of historical significance whose traces will not have disappeared even after many ages have passed".

7. Cabbages

Everyone knows how Edith Cavell was freed by the German Revolution and how that Revolution failed because of SPD treachery and the absence of a large, disciplined, organised revolutionary party. She resorted to new pseudonyms, moving from hotel to hotel, the White Terror coming closer, closer. In cafés and restaurants she met with the leaders of the groups of fighting workers and ate cabbage soup, fighting down memories of the cabbage fields of Norfolk, continuing to agitate, to struggle, to campaign ...

At 9 pm on 15 January 1919 she and Karl Liebknecht were arrested at 53 Mannheimer Strasse in Wilmersdorf and taken to the Eden Hotel and questioned. Did she remember her striking description of "the iron tools of murder"? Soldier Runge clubbed Liebknecht with his rifle butt, and the revolutionary was then put in a car, taken away and shot. Edith Cavell was beaten up by soldiers in the hotel lobby, then taken outside, where her skull was smashed by soldier Runge. She was put in a car and driven away into the night, shot in the head and dumped in the Landwehr Canal. The leaders of the SPD – Braun, Schmmidt, von Blair – were pleased at the news.

8. Carrots

How do I know all this? Because of the diary kept by my tattooed grandfather Albert, who was seduced by Rosa Luxemburg when he was a young patient in the Shoreditch Infirmary. Their relationship reached the point at which she told him everything about her past – and then their affair ended, because of his infidelity with a Glaswegian. In later years he would probably have largely forgotten about "Edith Cavell" had it not been for all the fuss that was made when she was caught by the Germans and shot. My grandfather wrote that Rosa Luxemburg told him when she first saw Edith Cavell she was nibbling a carrot, and that Edith cried out with a fiery glint in her eyes, "My favourite vegetable!" – an anecdote I have the gravest of doubts about. Everything else in this strange saga, however, rings true. There is a curious twist to this story which I shall include in case it has some bearing upon the infamous laws of motion of capitalism. After the war, while paying his respects to Rosa at the monument to her outside the National Portrait Gallery, my grandfather was struck on the shoulder by a small runner bean. A week later, standing silently by Luxemburg's grave in the grounds of Norwich cathedral, he suffered a painful blow from a small potato which came from nowhere and hit him in the neck. Foolishly, he then went off to Berlin to visit the memorial to Edith Cavell in Friedrichsfelde Cemetery. It was 21 April, 1929. A frozen carrot the size of a sledge-hammer plummeted from a cloudless sky and hit him on the head. He died instantly.

9. Radishes

On January 20th, 1902, seventeen years before her assassination, Edith Cavell threw a dinner party for Arthur Stadthagen, the Esiners and the three Kautskys. Mrs Eisner brought her a gift: a coloured photograph of the Eisner family in a beautiful gold frame. How charming! Thanks awfully!

Stadthagen was late, the rest tucked in. To drink? Lemonade or beer. To eat? Rolls with caviar, salmon and eggs, borsch with sausage-stuffed rolls, fish in sour sauce, steak with vegetables, compote.

What – no champagne? They laughed. Poking fun at the bleakness of revolutionary socialism. Edith smiled back. But of course! Producing, to their surprise, a bottle. They made silly faces, emptied it in no time.

Then dessert, cheese with radishes, black coffee with cognac. A wonderful evening!

But Jogiches was not amused. He wrote back from Zürich, sending critical comments about the radishes. Radishes with cheese! Whoever heard of such a thing!

Perhaps not in Russia. But in Germany radishes are served *only* with cheese, *after* dinner.

A wonderful evening? Why shouldn't socialists drink champagne and eat wonderful meals? Laughter, banter, vegetables, Marxism. Wonderful people, the Kautskys! But you have to be careful. Two years earlier Karl Kautsky asked for her help. He wanted her assistance in transcribing the fourth volume of *Das Kapital*. Kautsky said that after Engels' death there were only two people left in the world who could read Marx's handwriting: Eduard Bernstein and himself. *He wants to initiate me into Marx's hieroglyphs*, she wrote. Kautsky (1854-1938) told her of his anxiety that he would die unexpectedly, the work unfinished. But Edith shrewdly deduced that there was more to it than that: what Kautsky really wanted was someone who would do all the hard work, all the copying. And without a word of acknowledgement either; a vast, time-consuming, silent contribution to Marxism.

Not likely! *I assured him it would be pointless to teach me Marx's handwriting, since my chances of a sudden death are the same as his.*

The years judder by. And Kautsky? A sophist stripping Marxism of its revolutionary living spirit! Backsliding, spinelessness, subservience to opportunism and unparalleled vulgarisation of the theories of Marxism! Kautsky, like a schoolmaster who has become as dry as dust from quoting the same old textbooks on history, persistently turns his back on the twentieth century! A chewer of rags in his sleep. A chewer of borsch and sausage-rolls, of cheese and radishes.

And radishes,

as Lenin knew,

as Cavell learned too late,

are the most dangerous vegetables of all.

Angel

Out went the lights, off went the music blasting from the rooftop speakers, the two electric heaters began to die, they'd cut the power now, as earlier the phone. The wooden ladder lying across the floor, rectangles of dusty green carpet, four broken swivel chairs, a couple of plastic ones, a table. Graffiti everywhere.

KEEP YOUR SILENCE TO YOURSELF

THE BLISSFUL FOREST OF RADICAL SUBJECTIVITY

THE AXIOM "HONEST MEN HAVE NOTHING TO FEAR
FROM THE POLICE" IS UNDER REVIEW
BY THE AXIOMS APPEAL BOARD

ALL MOTORISTS ARE POTENTIAL KILLERS
NO JUSTICE JUST US

Outside, in the street, by the barricade of tyres, a lull, the four locked-on protesters prone in the road, arms deep in pipes, mattresses cut away from under them, ringed by clusters of police in riot gear, sheriff's officers, bailiffs.

"Take comfort," Angel had said, slipping his warm damp arm along her shoulders. "The next Labour Government will look very hard at the whole question of executions. We will review the situation, have no fear! *We will set up a committee to look into every aspect.* Of course, some executions are popular and it would be unwise to go against the will of the electorate. But in the case of your sister ... A posthumous pardon might very well be on the cards. A cheering thought, is it not?"

On the unreal cold unravelling night of Monday 28th November 1994, in the front bedroom of 66 Claremont Road, London E11, long ago it seemed, that morning, that morning when the city of Winchester lay amidst its convex and concave downlands on all the brightness and warmth of a July day, a blue July sky she could not forget, would never forget, in the pale awful unreal sky a few faint wisps of melting cirrus, while in the city the first tourists waited (she imagined) at the Information Centre for the start of the first guided tour or paid to enter the Heritage Centre in Upper Brook Street or queued for the Royal Hampshire Regiment Museum on Southgate Street or the nearby Royal Hussars Museum or the Royal Greenjackets Museum on Romsey Road or entered the Cathedral in order to pause above Jane Austen's grave and mouth deferential whispers combining in uninteresting combinations empty banalities and marble-smooth bourgeois platitudes.

Behind the city swept the rotund upland of St Catherine's Hill; further off, landscape beyond landscape, till the horizon was lost in the radiance of the sun hanging above it.

So cold. Dark. Police with Alsatians in the cemetery the other side of the Central Line. Time passing. A compressor is brought up, is parked outside. A drill. They can't get the locked-on four out. They are going to have to drill around them and dig them out. Slowly, slowly.

And that far gone July morning in a lay-by on the A33 two people sat silently in a parked scarlet Porsche. She could see herself, him, as in a movie. The young woman distracted, agitated, silent. Staring fixedly at a digital clock on the luxury polished walnut dashboard. The man brushing his fingers over the calfskin binding of the book. Periodic gusts softly rocking the car on its suspension as five-axle juggernauts blasted by.

Seven two three. Seven three four. Seven four five. Seven five zero. Her hot heart wildly grinding, achingly, uncontrollable, in pain. Seven five one. Seven five two. Her head metallic. Seven five three, seven five four. Feeling sick. A thick rising nausea, a swell of yesterday's bread and soup, yesterday's bacon. That bowl of shredded wheat. Seven five five, five six, five seven, five eight, five nine –

"No," she whispers, fists clenched, knuckles white, then louder, "No! NO! NO!"

And then: "Barbarians! Murdering capitalist barbarians!"

"Take comfort," Angel had said, slipping his warm damp arm along her shoulders. "The next Labour Government will look very hard at the whole question of executions. A committee –"

'Liza-Lu, shivering, feverish, throws open the door. Spews, copiously. Surge upon surge of vomit. A classic custard-yellow. Gets it out of her, all of it.

And Tess dead.

No, not in a Porsche.

As in the book, reaching the first milestone. The black flag moving slowly up the staff.

'Liza-lu's once-green eyes a bloodshot scarlet blaze. "Capitalism –" she begins to say.

Halted by Angel's yelp. And what a yelp! A piercing spreading yelp, a thing of high tinny screechings rising from a bed of old crisp rust, a loose ever-slackening spool of thin yellowish squealings, a yelp of melded squeaks redolent of mice and ambitious stoats.

The pale watery blood drains from Angel's smooth wax cheeks, he shuts his eyes tight (his weasel eyes, his obsequious sly slippery eyes), reaches out for a brick wall to lean against, the solid reliable wall of a bank not there in the book, clamps the palms of his hands tightly over his ears, his face wearing the anguished expression of a man still in the harsh dark troubling iron swell of last winter's constipation.

"Capitalism," she begins again – then mistakes constipation for incomprehension.

Sighs. Remembers Angel's limitations. His cosmic ignorance. After all, he'd only ever been a barrister and a pop singer. *Angel Blair and His Modern Wind Orchestra*, comprising a tin whistle, a hollow-sounding drum, and three distorted tubas loaned by the Nellcock Estate (Angel, of course, blew his own trumpet). They made babbly-bubbly, empty chug-a-lug music. Hoping to be big as the Beatles, say, or Garth Brooks. The *Penge Gazette* compared them to Abba and forecast greatness. Ending up smaller than Simon Dupree and the Big Sound.

"Bourgeois economists," she says, disgustedly lifting his arm as you would a dead lizard, "regard capitalism as an eternal and natural form of production, rather than an *historical* form of production. They then attempt to legitimize it by formulating the conditions of its becoming as the conditions of its contemporary realisation! The points at which the suspension of the present form of production relations gives signs of its becoming – foreshadowings of the future! Just as, on one side the pre-bourgeois phases appear as *merely historical,* i.e. suspended pre-suppositions, so do the contemporary conditions of production likewise appear as engaged in *suspending themselves* and hence in positing the *historic presuppositions* for a new state of society! At *an absolute minimum* socialism must start from a recognition that there are classes in society and that socialists stand with workers against the bosses and the powerful! – it must mean a belief that capitalism is not the best way to run things! – that there needs to be common ownership of the means of production and public planning!"

"No, no, no" Angel gasps, flinching. He staggers drunkenly to the right, crunches on a clove of garlic kept for just such emergencies, whirls his expensive jewel-studded little silver crucifix against the bats and fangs and threat. How he loathes hyphens and scarlet exclamation marks! How he respects asterisks and mist-white amnesia!

"That word," he whispers. "Never let me hear that word again. It is unseemly. Improper. Not nice." His head nods like a nodding dog's, a thing of regularity with a mock-velvet smirk at its axis.

"Yes," he reiterates, jabbing a smooth finger at nothing in particular. "Nice people do not use that word. Nice people *never* use that word. You will not go far in life if you go around using words like that, my dear. People will think you rather odd. You will be shunned. You will never become a secretary or be able to pursue a career in banking or get anywhere in law let alone become a parliamentary candidate if you persist – if you persist – if you persist ..."

He fizzles, gestures vaguely until his thumbs began to droop.

"Oh, piss off, Blair," 'Liza-Lu snaps, who has heard it all

before. "If you think you can fuck me just because you fucked Tess you've got another think coming, dickhead. I've never liked barristers, anyway. Besides ..."

She points to St Catherine's Hill, and beyond it the rolling green acres of Twyford Down. "Look. Over there. What was it Thomas Hardy wrote?"

Behind the city swept the rotund upland of St Catherine's Hill; further off, landscape beyond landscape, till the horizon was lost in the radiance of the sun hanging above it.

"See what's happening over there on the downs? Those lights on the hillside. Security lighting. Surveillance cameras. Private detectives. An army of security guards with a licence to rough-up protesters. Backed up by the scumbags of the Hampshire Constabulary. Hoddinott's henchmen. Yes, folks, that's the M3 extension. Straight through the Down! Unbelievable. This is the real face of Tory Britain. Carving up Twyford Down. In the name of Conservativism! What a fucking joke! What did the Conservatives ever conserve except corruption, privilege and the stinking class system? And their stocks and shares. And dividends from Tarmac. And contributions to the Party from Tarmac. And what's the Labour Party had to say about all this? Bugger all."

But Angel wasn't listening. How he remembers the defining moment of Ramsay MacDonald's life! That time in 1919 when, following a walk in the Cairngorms, the great Labour leader was obliged to kill time at a railway station and went to see what Menzies' bookstall had in stock. *We found it was being used for the dissemination of leaflets on "Direct Action". We took one and laughed and wept at its rubbish, invested in a Conrad, and so home to supper and bed.*

Angel straightened his tie, cleared his throat, combed his hair and made his position clear.

"I want a Labour Party that flatters to the vulture!" smoothly he said. "I want a fluke that labours to the party! I want a party that says and partly means what it cleverly can't and a party that means whatever while it says! I want Muzak where you work and Prozac while you walk! Less questions and upset

136

stomachs! Diazepam and Propranolol for all! The new constitution will state clearly what it states. A blandness in hinting at syrup! We need more starshine and moonbeams and a dynamic modern astronomy! Above all, we need gloss and shine! The shiniest, smoothest, lightest, gloss and shine we can find!"

He didn't seem to notice 'Liza-lu ebbing away.

She ebbed, he sped.

He sped along the fast lane of motorways and rose into the air in elevators with glass walls. Now he was important. Now his molars shone in the dark. His platform rhetoric was flowing and sparkly as tinsel. He was popular with sheep, chameleons and scarabs. At small local meetings he was passionate and assertive and spoke fiercely of his deep concern about the doings of Conservatives. With journalists he was cautious and careful, emphasising the need for pragmatism and moderation. In the past, he said, Labour had been too economistic. He called for a revival of unselfish, non-material socialism. In off-the-record briefings he blamed the long-term unemployed for the budgetary crisis. He let it be known that there were too many rowdy six-year-olds in society and that prison might be the only answer. He attacked single mothers for their unnatural and anarchic way of life. He backed the Los Angeles police one-hundred-per-cent. He made it clear that change would only ever come through Parliamentary speeches. He was vehemently opposed to all strikes for the damage they did to Labour's electoral prospects. On Sundays he worshipped at the Bank of England. He was made a Privy Councillor and relished his meetings with the Queen. Like Ramsay MacDonald he went away from the Palace feeling he had taken part in something very much like Holy Communion. He had a house in Islington, a villa in Spain, a cottage in the Yorkshire Dales. He owned more than two hundred copies of *James Ramsay MacDonald: Labour's Man of Greatness,* three of them signed. Mirrors adored him. In them he smoothed his hair, his smile, his words. He performed major monologues in the bright bathroom, the crisp mint odour of toothpaste holding back the faint far reek of foul, yellowish-black turds. "The task of socialism," he told his nasal hair trimmer," is to modify the fabric of society, to make government the greatest of the arts." He was tough with the towel rail, facing up fair and square to its scarlet and purple pattern: "We would have to examine that, obviously, because there are questions of costs." He did not flinch in the face of the spider plant, warning it that its demands could only ever be introduced sensibly and flexibly. "There is no room for complacency!" he advised the banana hair conditioner. "We must get to grips with criminal youth!" he yelped at the pink tablet of soap, squeezing it 'til it shot out through the louvre window and hit a passing delinquent. Alone with the toilet roll he freely confessed he had no axe to grind. The rubber duck he briskly warned against folly, advising it that it was time to get round the negotiating table. Lotions and warm water lapped his heart. Submerged in froth, he played with his slogans.

MORE OF WHATEVER YOU'D LIKE THAT'S
POPULAR AND NICE WITH ANGEL BLAIR

OPPORTUNITY. SUNNY VISIONS. PLEASANTNESS.
WOULDN'T IT BE GOOD?
VOTE LABOUR

BUSINESS BRITAIN. MODERATE JELLY.
SENSIBLE MEDIUM FLAVOURS.
ALL WITH
NEW IMPROVED LABOUR

HUNDREDS OF DREAM FLIGHTS
WITH NEWER, NICER LABOUR

In a speech to pink attentive businessmen including executives from Informa Tech, GKN, GEC-Marconi, Wimpey, McDonnell Douglas, Siemens, VSEL, Ferranti, Tate & Lyle, Tarmac, Vosper Thornycroft, the Chemical Industries Association and

Scottish Nuclear, he was plainspoken and tough. "I did not launch this debate because it was the easy thing to do but because it was the shiny thing to do!"

Bluntly and boldly he told them of the need to end welfare dependency and put the shirkers back to work in the cabbage fields of Suffolk. Given the malaise among the workshy, amputation of limbs could not be ruled out. But disability could not be an excuse for laxity. Stilts and ponies would be supplied to ensure a continuing supply of window-cleaners. A minimum wage would only be set after consultation with top entrepreneurs. Parity with Chinese slave labourers would be introduced only if it could be shown that this would avoid any adverse impact on jobs. He could not help hearing their whispers, their admiration. *A statesmanlike moderation of tone ... A first-class parliamentarian ... A sound grasp of the issues ...*

On the way in to dinner he continued. "Democracy! Opportunity! Visions! Green traffic lights! Somewhere safe to park! I am writing to the Prime Minister demanding assurances that he is legislating in the national interest, not merely attempting to score political points!"

He never noticed when 'Liza-lu slipped away. As for Tess – he'd forgotten her after the first canapé.

"This slice of roast tenderised diseased beef is delicious!"

His elegant second wife, Plum, was beside him, wearing her favourite trouser-suit. She radiated charm and insincerity. Her shoulder pads discharged several thousand volts if touched by a Poll Tax defaulter. She had shares in cattle-ranching, chicken slurry and quarries. She was hard as nails and one of the finest bum-bailiffs of her generation.

Before he made his speech she led him into a private room. She had a surprise for him.

"Look, Angel!" she said, smiling. "Our family."

Goodness! Three (or was it two?) delightful children. The boy (or boys) freckled and mischievous, the girl (or girls) shy and eyelash-fluttery. "Now no one can ever doubt your hetero-sexuality," Plum cried gaily.

She beckoned to the photographers, thin, scruffy, obsequious men in leather jackets, who addressed him as "luv" and fussed about exposures and light. A young woman powdered his cheeks and pencilled a wholesome rouge across his lips. Drenched in flashes, he kept up his blank smile for as long as was required. When the photographers had gone Plum seized the children by the arm and forced them back into their box. Their muffled cries she extinguished with pillows, gags and a brisk thrashing.

Angel looked a little sulky. He frowned at the box. "Do we *have* to have them about the house?"

Plum was astonished. "Of course not, darling! I've arranged for them to be transported on a regular basis to the Institute of Jesuit Pederasts. They'll only be around at bedtime and for photo-opportunities."

"Thank goodness for that."

Pausing for a few seconds in order to wolf down a silver plateful of jellied frogs' legs, bisque of fennel and horseradish with fine herbs, goose liver with truffle and pistachio and a generous bucketful of Charlotte Malakoff aux Fraises, he began his speech.

"Let me make it clear that the trade unions will have no special and privileged place in the next Labour government! Our first obligation will be to tyranipocrisy in whatever form it manifests itself. We must all tighten our belts. We promise no penal rates of tax for hard-working multi-millionaires! Instead of outdated dogmas about common ownership we will abase ourselves on the four pillars of opportunity and the seven pillars of Norman's wisdom! We will abuse ourselves on the thirteen pillar-boxes of Penge! We stand for the five pillworts of responsibility! The nineteen pilules of fairness! The eighteen piltocks of trust! And above all else, a plethora of pustule-coloured pilot-balloons, in tribute to Commissioner Nellcock!" *(Prolonged applause.)*

Touring the Esher death factory he jangled some cuffs, caressed some prods, gazed admiringly at the nosecones and silver exports. He'd long forgotten 'Liza-lu. He knew nothing of how she'd followed John Keats to that dry chalky down where the air was once worth six pence a pint and where instead of lambs bleating from hilly bourn she'd met razor wire and Group 4 security guards with video cameras and employees of Brays Detective Agency and the Hampshire Constabulary and huge crawler bulldozers weighing 132 tonnes capable of pushing 50 cubic metres of aggregate with a single 20-tonne ripper tooth to grind into the Twyford chalk and split it open, after which came the diesel-engined yellow big wheel loaders emitting carcinogenic particulates while the 30-cubic-metre bucket filled 200-tonne dump trucks in just four loads and where she, 'Liza-lu Durbeyfield, had been punched by security guards, videoed by Group 4, wrongfully arrested for "obstruction" by a pair of blue-uniformed yobs, roughly thrown into the back of a Transit van, imprisoned and injuncted and imprisoned again and sued for damages by the Department of Transport on the basis of information supplied by the private detective agency. Damages! As if it wasn't *the Department of Transport* that was committing criminal damage on a stupendous, spreading scale!

In the footsteps of Keats, yes. John Keats, whose "Ode to Autumn" is set against outlying Winchester, the fields and water meadows and Twyford Down, a languorous soft landscape of brimming abundance on the brink of sagging decay, curiously prophetic, the fume of poppies now drenched by the funnelled blue polluting fumes from fifty thousand M3 exhausts. John Keats, whose last night in England was spent at an isolated mill-house amid the flat wastes of shoreline at Bedhampton – a shoreline blasted in the nineteen-sixties by the building of the A27 dual carriageway (Keats's plaque just visible as you drive by). A nation in thrall to the tyranny of the car; Keats's world – Hardy's, too – gone forever. And in Dorchester, on 5 August 1994, the demolition workers began to smash down the old workhouse, the one where Fanny Robin died, to make room for a new car park ...

Like Keats in September 1819, she'd gone from Winchester to Walthamstow. Here she crashed out with friends who lived on Lime Street, in the very house once lodged in by William Morel. It was just a short bike ride to the proposed route of the M11 Link Road. *That* struggle was just beginning and she was there from the start, the sunlit march from Wick Field to the South Woodford to Barking Relief Road, culminating in a sit-down on the dual carriageway when the police wouldn't allow them to walk as far as the roundabout, as well as on that first bleak day when the houses by the footbridge on Eastern Avenue were occupied, a struggle that had led from the pushing down of the fences around George Green to the wet dark windswept morning the police had come to take the old chestnut tree, from Wanstonia to Leytonstonia, from Bush Wood to Euphoria, and finally to Claremont Road, where a grey cold dawn was breaking, while the riot police patrolled in the street below and the private detectives snapped her with their telephoto lenses, and time coldly passed, dragging slowly on until the inevitable moment when the bailiffs came through the window ...

On the Saturday she went back to look. It began to rain. The tower dismantled, the entire street bulldozed to rubble, the trees clipped back and bare. Gone. Including the corrugated iron fence where someone had painted in big red letters *"No, no!" said the Queen. "Sentence first – verdict afterwards"*, together with Alice's reply.

She pedalled back to Lime Street in the rain.

Someone had put the TV on in the front room. As she entered she glanced at the screen. There he was, yet again, every hair in place, lips ruby red, with powdered cheeks, Angel Bodger Charles Derek Ethelred Frederick Gordon Herbert Ingmire Julian Knowall Lynton Mordor Nigel Oliver Poulson Quigly Rupert Simon Timothy Ugley Viscount Wyntle Xavier Yapper Blair. "Instead of bowing to outdated dogmas about common ownership," he was saying in a calm, measured monotone, "we will abase ourselves on the four pillars of opportunity, we will –"

She sat down on the sofa, with closed eyes and half believed herself at Twyford once again. Waist-high grasses rustling in the wind, green landscape beyond green landscape, the horizon lost in radiance, specks of darting swallows high overhead. Then evening's shadow darkened the slopes like nightfall in the tropics, a sudden darkness propelling her to that cold room at Claremont, while riot police and bailiffs swarmed in the street.

"The trade unions will have no special and privileged place in the next Labour government! Our first obligation will be to tyranipocrisy in whatever form it —"

"Bah!" thought 'Liza-lu, getting up. She switched the set off, reducing Angel Blair to a sudden shrinking grey pinprick that vanished under a surface blankness of plastic and dust. "YOU'RE NOTHING BUT A PACK OF CARDS!"

Paper Heart (a story in three albums)

Planet Waves

"Who are you? Where you been? Where you going?" Headlights against the sky, headlights coming over the hill, down the road, screech of brakes. "What you doin' here?" The hard-eyed frowning cop's questions that empty road night in Norfolk. What, where, who? *What's happening?* The Headquarters boys putting the pressure on. Who? The name's Hawkins. He wasn't doing anything, not that winter. Walking along the verge, no street-lights or cityglow, twenty-six years old, same as Keats, and the Van Gogh incandescent stars sparkly-shimmering, iced-up inside. Afterwards recalled as one of the bleakest of bleak winters. Mister Hawkins was living at The Patch, rat-sized hole under the front door, on the dole, sense of emptiness, of going no place & nowhere, crapping unremarkable dull brown crap while the rain beat down always & always on the murky skylight, ancient hissing boiler and rooms with old striped wallpaper, grey bed of the Polaroid fun and the quick Bianco screw, big old multi-tenanted house on the Norwich road, the death of the heart and the rotting stables out the back where the lidless dustbins dribbled soggy girly magazines & dragon-mouth Heinz cans. Huge padlock hung inside the iron staple, green mould covered the wood of the fence and of the gates, a dark wide entrance hall, communal stairs from the last century & a cold breeze blowing as from a cellar. From the hall he got up the stairs, sloven, swaying, worn lino, scraps of brown dark threadbare carpet, cut off from everything, like being stuck inside a crumby little town in the nineteenth century dead heart of a plain in Russia, dread defunctive days where the colour all drained to the steel of the sea and the mud of the cliffs, the rain beating down down down on the skylight, overwhelming him, the waves breaking on the empty winter shingle, the crumbling cliffs with the half houses, split homes, wallpaper exposed to the rain & gulls, the gull mobs screeching in the blank sky, empty sea, & the songs matched everything, sense of nostalgia, winter, snow flurries across the cliffs, *ennuyé,* sparks of rage, hatred, fashed by a gash & anxious to be out of all this, desperate, the rancour, the grey bitter bed and that sobbing sour day, wizened months, bricked-up, the boredom piled on boredom, and desperate to be going, to be going, to be gone.

Desire

Lo and behold! 747 high over the Prairies, high over the Rockies, crawling over the planet to another world. To the library, the high tower. The papers. O bright and breezy day! O hot spicy rapturous season of Carnival and Masks! Flax and fire. Ooooooooh! Sweet beginnings. Pulling over at night, the airport across the sound. Navigation lights gliding in the sky, rising, dropping. 747s, coming and going. Coming. On tenter-hooks, Mister Hawkins and Mrs Mozart! Staring at each other wildly, her widow's nails digging into his arm. Kindling eyes, the blood's lava. Flax, fire, growing fond, fonder, fondling, growing ... The pulse a blaze, dark eyes darting light. Firstkiss. Moist gorgeous filtrum. Clasping grasping clenching pulling and pooling and suck. In ferment! Astray! Wild sweet attunement, each kiss a heart-quake. Bare feet hurrying bed-ward, covers that won't turn back fast enough. Lo, in flames in a crack, behold flax fork flesh and forefinger and all the burning tongues. Fleshly meddle, on to the forfended place, ferret and firk! Impaled by motes, speared by fire, rolling among blizzards of gold. One flesh. Broken words and burning tongues, days of gold in an iron age. Stark white fritillary basking on a black stone outside München, broken glass at the Strand Palace Hotel! Cream pastries in St. Anton, reckless scented morning in Seattle! Frisky lambs in Derwentwater pastures, burning snow on the slopes of Wenatchee! Sweet morning in Tongue! A hot liaison under the huge cotton sheets, fiery dust amidst Ottawa's drifts and ice, and the sparkling stars their nuptial torches. Splashing in the pool at the Chateau Laurier! Raspberry smear on the carpet attracting the granite blonde chambermaid's harsh comment in Zell! The moons rolled on. Frenzied agonizing rush! Hot whirling motel-hotel season of nimble tongue and castanets, blazing eye and tingling nose, skilled finger and burning marshland delta. Trembling Mister Hawkins thrice plunging the scooped squirming electric widow. Stirred, stirring, sweetness, lapping lips and fingerstrokes, gash wet & pupils hot & dark, arrow-head mouthed, go gentle, gentle, lingering-out, quivering, tenderness-frenzy, speech rapid & vehement, plough and die, clasp and buckle, buck and flood, shudder, discharges stupendous, meltings, sticky angels, earthless, plummeting. Then again. So quite new a thing. Bodies, a body. What it does, its hows, spine and bone and the trembling, the slow stroking, the thrill. Clouds of marsh fragrance, rolling. Swelling organ, seas of flame. Come and go, go and come, here, there and – Taking flight, hopping landscapes, crossing borders, time zones, continents. Over dunes of sand and snow, covering a lot of territory that year. Haste and glare and glitter. Mister Hawkins at the opera. Goggled Mister Hawkins on skis, twenty-eight, zig-zagging the dazzling blanks. Mister Hawkins on Wreck Beach. Mister Hawkins depositing a fertile soft & chocolate coloured trail. Mrs Mozart hoisting her skirt and pissing on leafmould in the grounds of Cawdor Castle. Mister Hawkins freshening up at the Oregon Memory Motel, watching a TV evangelist. Bare-assed Mister Hawkins & the electric widow rocking among the ancient ferns. Mister Hawkins and the widow with Johann in Bent's basement. Delighted eyes, Mister Hawkins hand-in-hand with Mrs Mozart by the spangled summer lake & happy so happy. Oh chymic treasure! Oh wine-sharp and honey-still warp of tideless joyous morning, oh golden juiced Cantata afternoons. Rocking with the widow among the pines, yes! Look at it loom there, Thing that she ... Pumped-up, quivering. Trumpets out of a blue morning, floorfucks, fernfucks, miraculous basement afternoons, bedsheet slimed with grey, and next day's dry, coin-sized blotches. Rustlings, murmurings, sucking, licking, high voltage sweats and spurts, rejoin rejoice separate and rejoin, separate, spent, nightblur of slippingawayfatigue, jam on cock, honey on crotch and breasts, cushioned by warm thudding ribs, tumbling to voluptuous slumbers, the big voluptuous slumber as a dying might be, should be.

Hard Rain

Torpor, lassitude. Blossoms fallen, sap gone. Moon still bright, revels long ended. Gone, wallop. Passed away, thrown away. Cut and dried. Phantoms and dust, echoes. Put it down in the end, all of it, eh? What's over, over. A September chill in the air, the mountains and the seas between. Narrow England again. Fizzles in Finchley, then off. North past the cooling towers, mind cascading, low raggy middle-grey clouds scud the white sky, trainload of metallically smart salesmen & the track muttering *no home to go to, no home to go to, no home to go to*. Singular vicissitudes, oh yes. Mister Hawkins, older now, lost in the backwash, throbbing heart and a blurred drugged look to him, a thoughts-against-thoughts thoughts-elsewhere expression, rueful, dressed in an old Oxfam overcoat crossing the bridge on the retreat from Moscow, to the far platform and out, yellow-tinted ancient walls. Cold and getting colder, September ending, walk on greyheart across the black footbridge beside the line, river below high & fast, city background of strange smoky phosphorescent half world. Sorely tried and sadly changed. Motley's the only wear. Disowned, so to speak. Forsaken and forlorn. All amort. Absence inconspicuous, nobody can tell what he – A new place to dwell. Living in obscurity, on very small means. Leading a sort of soundless, inert life. An out-of-the-way street; the flat dilapidated. Domestic desolation in a little room. To end in languor. Empty skies, scumbled greys, drizzle. The grey signal flag. Fall's bleak beginning. Mister Hawkins enters the lit house, climbs up the narrow winding stairs, slips a coin in the meter. Lassitude, torpor. All day in the rocker. The ticking in the walls, the sapless cinders. Eyes resolutely cast down, fingers twining and untwining themselves restlessly in lap. The clenched fist. Day and night. Not one minute in an hour, no. When his throbbing

147

heart; when he did not – No, not one minute. Immured in a
little room. Dawdling discordant Sundays, travesties of blem-
ished time. Tea-cup with a crack in it. And how would you
describe Mister Hawkins? What sort of mood did he seem to
be in? Condition of atrophied coma, alas. Cumbered by coils;
wrung out; selfstrung. Arachnoid, buried above ground. Alone
in the snivelling hours. The voice barely audible, a thin,
stretched, barbed whisper. Quis-quae-quae croak. With slower
and slower articulation. Speech failing. A wintery summary.
Old, cold, grey. Pallid. Smell of parboiled cauliflower and
greasy bacon, dead cigarettes, cold ashtrays, sinkfull of greasy
plates and smeared tarnished cutlery beneath the pale shallow
silent scum. Mute nights, darkled defunctive days. The no-
colour void. Mornings of deep, desolating emptiness. Mornings
when all the heartstrings like wild horses pull ... Not even in
Utah, no. Cold laughter, dead laughter. The sound of distant
barking heard from Maryon Park. The reckoning. Life's strange
principle lying deep and the yellow leaf everywhere. By a
guttering candle, gutted, clawed, taken aback, lying aback &
broken, half-sodden, washed by stale and detritus, tipped in
Time's gutter, turns, gets onto his knees, falls back. The
sediment. The inner weight. The unknown thing. The impulse
to... No continuance. His old desire to – Preparing to leave all
this; preparing to leave ... Going out, once or twice, nowhere
really. Scuffed suede shoes. Takes a walk, yes. Down the old
familiar street. Hotel neon flashing blue, crimson, blue.
Chocolate the colour of shit, from an automatic machine.
Bread tasteless, biscuits of sand. Cigarettes, flat warm beer.
The afternoons of the dying year steadily shortening. Then
back up the narrow winding stairs. A fool whose bells have
ceased to ring at all. Fingers beating the wall in time to an old
tune. Into sleeping bag. Stone age, age of iron and scrap.
Stretched out, on his stomach, dead to the world. Frail, frailer.
Mumbles as he turns. Face buried in the pillow. Dead face
nightly appearing. Cramped in every limb. Barely a breath.
Buried in the broken mine. Drowned, bloated on the black
lake's rubbish-littered bed. Smashed and swallowed by an

avalanche. Sweating in a bed-roll. Delving the dead days. Delving with stone fingers the black depths, the unending silence. Ice blocks. Eyes that have stared too long stare at the wedge of light at the end of an unwarmed room. Speared by a slash of soupy light, in a moment dissolved. The residue. The no-colour void. Become a ghost, a meagre transparency. Mausoleum mornings, graveyard afternoons. The verdigris. Dead up-ended stiff-leg robin on the pale verge, saplings broken. *Elle vous suit par tout.* Days brimming with deadness and darks. Hands plunged in cloudy water, up to the wrist. Dullness and cold glasses, dreary evenings, congealed beerfroth. Scatter all away, dead nights washing away, down, down the drain. Called it dead winter of plucked cabbage stalks, dead monuments and toad-dark carpets, ubiquitous mist. Those selfsame months of the soulful Pole's hit symphony. Hawkins, his discomposure bleakly evident, composes nothing, else unsent letters, abandoned stanzas, lists, rolls in a sleeping roll on a kitchen floor, a mouse patters over his heart and he wakes shrieking. Numbness, pins and needles. Hangovers. Bubbles of bitterness. Notices a strange shape – una extraña forma – his shirt's all torn and filthy – y sucia mi camisa – and, and, and. And so on and so on and so on. *Ah riedi ancora qual eri allora* and all that jive. By what ravaged, by what blanched? The punishing wind's frost fingers making him shiver enclosed though he was by layers of blackness. Steam rising from pockmarked lugubrious urinals. Scourged by the sting and rip of petty, poisoned minutes, impossible to think, concentrate. Bolted; captived; speaks to dead walls. Time so slow, you'd think it had stopped for bad & all, tepid November, perilous dead December, barren January, bitter torpid February. A long and snake-like life. The long year linked with heavy day on day. The black empty nest in the dead ash filling with grey snow. The bathroom down the stairs, subterranean dull green walls, shitting pellets, dark cartridges, in an ill humour. Up and down Bootham, past the Auden plaque. Up and down, down and up. Down, down, down. Down and desperate. Desperate, getting out of the city in a hired car alone, crashing the gears, through dale and doleful valley. Empty rainswept hillside carpark. Moor barren, seeing the farm faraway in the cup of the bleak vale. A high, desolate place where the mountains came crashing down and crumbled at his feet. Wrinkles, the first grey hairs. The blur and crumble of great hearts failing. A day spent walking among ruins. His need naked, his mind spinning dizzy into rages of space, wanting to be gone. Back to the city to face the musty corridors of a crooked year, the indictment, the gradual disremembering. Mister Hawkins watching his step; circumscribed Mister Hawkins on the dole, dealing in morsels again. His München-pain and madness and all the dahlias in the sooty garden undulating in Munchpainwaves, raw sienna ribbed and shivering. Poor drudge engulfed in sleet, shivering in the drifts of his need. Madly blind. Bereft. Sans everything. Briars, brambles. In a dark obscure wood perplexed. The sear, the yellow leaf. Heart-stopping shots nearby, and the burrs, the burrs. Everything grey, shrunk and shrivelled. As turns the needle – Bearings lost and bleakness unrelenting until – Until the coming back. Back to Hellfire Corner and the long crawl through the chattering mud. The impulse ... No continuance. Butterflies. Then the impulse again. Doggedly pulling back the covers, then pulling them stiffly forward again. No continuance. Then motion, motions. Definite circumgyratory movements! Then total collapse. Utter fatigue. A trail of cartoon zeds swimming from nose to ceiling. Then close-up of eyes opening. Heavy eyes. Baggy eyes. Eyes dying. Dead marble. Stone. Stone eyelids lowered, voice like gravel. The long grass growing above his burnt out brain. A ruin. Fractured, fragmented, broken. Cold-pinched. In a pretty pickle. Picking up the pieces, pooling stagnant resources, pulling his selves together. Cigarette, flaring match. Trickle of smoke. Speechless. In thought, deeper. Thinking, stupidly, to come through the waste, the hazard ... Barren fabulation. Paralysed by poetry, the pelting rain. Killer words, late Beethoven. Melancholy and whisky, Bach and solitude, empty house, derelict factory that Sunday, Balmacaan ruin, margarine, eggs, fist-fucking phantoms, *Hamlet*, Kees. String Quartet No. 13 played beside a whale carcase rotting on a rainy beach. Call him pitiful, helpless. Old leather-back turtle, in torment. Forget-me-nots brittle in an old book. Obliterated mornings, obliterated nights. The motes showering Mister Hawkins slumped drunk, soft interminable tread of the long gone, odd specks and flakes in the wall mirror. The first mysterious lines of age turning a human face into an old, wretched, used-up thing, a child's puzzled eyes staring out of the ruin. Out there, through the blear pane, time accelerating. Yellow fields, sparkly starlings, children pouring brightly out of school. This is how the story ended, is it, in dribs & drabs? Dazed, done in mentally and the money running out. Considerations pinching his heart, lack of breath, Mister Hawkins getting fat and sluggish. Thinks: how quiet everything is. This could go on forever. This is what it is to die. Rain, days, liquor, a dripping tap; the store laid away for a monotonous future being eaten away. Another beer, another slug. And another. Remembering the dead rat below the clear water at the very edge of the loch. Thwarted by language, class and money. Born in a Yorkshire mist, dying in one. Remembering, disremembering, having come this far, twenty-nine. No! in drizzle. Call it between-times. Call it coming slowly back to what's imminent and real. Lukewarm radiators, tired animals, crooked neighbours, the finny people slow-circling in bowls and tanks, erasers, foliage leaking laughter, the sad and quiet weddings, name tags, milk, gunsights, complete strangers, digits, guitars and sugared alm-onds. Apples, melons. Flowers and herbs. Coping with what vanishes and never returns. Bodies, names, empires, gone in a puff of smoke. Rushing, pointlessly, after the melting drifts. Exhausted, coming back. To life. To start afresh! A forward course for Mr What's-your-name. Face growing eager, yes. Brightening into a smile. More. Feverish eagerness, breathless interest. Sunny side up on the sun-sun-sunny side o' the street. Kiki Dee and Elton John and "True Love", Terry Evans singing "That's The Way Love Turned Out For Me". The good things that make it all so – Children's laughter. Roses, daisies, sun dried tomatoes. Mixed herbs and Chablis and Aberdeen Angus. Cigarettes and sex, beers and fondling. How's things? Dripping lips; trickles, splashes. Luscious clusters. Okay, I guess. So-so. "At five? I'd love to. Pretty well. And you?" Putting your finger on it. Putting it in, putting it down in the end, all of it. Yes. Back again. Pause, rest for a while. Not, perhaps, time wasted. *Listen to me.* Shaping at that table between his hands, the story. Setting it down, an incomplete thing. Dreams, too. The inmates. A globe of glass, cracked. From the first capital to the last period. Literary concupiscence! Monosyllabic invention! Sheets of sorrow. In his old lunes again. Turning a distich. In paper-durance bound. One sustained frenzied agonizing rush. Lines, circles, scenes, letters and characters. Words on words. The anaesthesia of them. The mist; the scorching; a little drop of ink and the tap-drip of desolate weeping. Soliloquies. Useless, helpless reiteration, elegies on brambles. Get a grip on your selves. The lines all running together. Paper heart where the lines are smudged, where the ink's bled. Yellowed, brittle. Zoo now I hope – Writing steadily on, pausing only to sit while his fingers rested. *The glow and the shadow, every scrap of memory, every remembered speech, every letter* ... To hold a farthing candle to the sun. A world of words! Cigarette scarring slowly into the edge of the rented table. Halts; half remembers. Crammed with observation, perishing fast. Burnt out by time and liquor. Down at zero. Then starts again. In fits and starts, in mangled forms, the visible lines. Fettered hand and foot by a little strip of inked ribbon. Motley-minded; getting more and more enmeshed, like a roach in a web. Memory's crupper. Rags and dust, rigmarole. As the torrent widens ... Tumult of recollections pressing upon his mind, frowns. Journeys through the bygone time. Shadows of shadows. Then remembers the cigarette, raises it to rub uselessly at the new scorch before – Open brackets: Ah, the pleasures of frottage. Perpend; close brackets. Seated placidly in shirt sleeves. Applying his mind. Keeping the atrocious reader in suspense. Reaching the end, at last, almost. To have done. Waste and idle papers. The words all fallen from his cracked lips, disfiguring the page's whiteness. Disclosures over. Past mastered, perhaps. Then raising his eyes, staring for a long time at the chipped cup, the steaming bowl. Go litel bok, go. Sipping the tea. Taking the bread, taking the spoon, beginning to eat.

Eating a little, three or four spoonfuls. Without appetite, head aching less now. Hearing the clock for the first time, its ticking filling the room. Raising his head, looking at the window. The York mists, the mists on the mountain hung. Dull aquarium glow, morning again. New morning! Tiptoeing to the door, quietly opening it a little. Going out. Stumbling, falling on grass, springing up. Chipper. Jaunty gait, cheery whistling. Passing through the passing day, the crucible, the petty dust. Not even in Utah, no. Cracked and smashed, dust. Gone, almost. The faintest of faint shadows, the merest echoes of echoes, fading, ebbing, almost gone. The lines running in the rain. The lines blown, smudged. A kind of sigh; things indecipherable. Eyes down, raised; alert for eyes of grey. Learning in which direction to turn, to turn and turn again. Congratulations! Have a nice day! And old paper heart goes on, goes on. To search. To search again for salmon singing in the street. Learning to walk once more. Pitter-patter, pitter-patter, old paper heart. Water in a gutter, burbling. Goes on. Then gone, almost. Almost gone. Gone.

To Wanstonia

And send imagination forth
Under the day's declining beam ...
W.B. Yeats, "The Tower"

A

A is for ABELARD and ACT and ADVENTURE and AGITATOR and ANONYMOUS and ANTIFORM and ARROOGA and AUTOBAHN and AVALANCHE ...

"What's happening?"

16 February 1994. Squatters in Cambridge Park made a determined and noisy last stand in their battle against the M11 link road. Self-declared Fort Wanstonia was protected by trenches and barriers including a Citroën 2CV which had been buried in a mud wall.

As dawn broke squatters relayed the message that traffic had stopped using the road and at 7 am coachloads of police were seen.

For two hours the houses were full of rumours and reports on the latest police activity. The campaigners sat in hallways singing word-changed songs including "I'm fixing a hole where the bailiff gets in", "They'll be coming through the windows when they come" and "Our house, in the middle of the siege."

"What's happening?"

22 January 1994, late morning and a fine English drizzle coming from a grey sky and settling on the silent bulldozers and cranes, making moist the barbed wire, the blood trickling down Gerard Manley Hopkins's shin from the slashed skin just below his right knee, his jeans torn, his anorak ripped, the skin torn on his right wrist too, a pleasing resemblance to stigmata, his fall through the wire recorded on video not once but twice,

154

the snouts of the cameras still moving, sniffing for intruders, somewhere in one of the buildings a bank of screens and a security guard gazing at the small grey image of the poet falling through the wire, while the sound of sirens grows louder, louder ...

*

Anonymous poem from the times of the enclosures:

The law locks up
The man or woman
Who steals the goose
From off the Common
But leaves the greater villain loose
Who steals the Common from the goose.

*

Anonymous letter, *Redbridge Guardian,* 3 March 1994:

I feel I must add to mounting comments concerning the recent "Battle of Wanstonia". I feel it's time we thanked the police and security guards for maintaining order – not an easy task when members of the Welling BNP riot were present.

*

"Construction of the State Autobahn is under way at 51 points across the country! Although the work has only just begun, already 52,000 men are labouring on building sites! A further 100,000 men are supporting them in the industries supplying materials and on bridge construction sites!"

Todt, at the Nazi Party's 1934 Nuremberg Rally.

*B is for BAILIFF and BUMBAILIFF and BULLY and
BARNARD and BUREAUCRACY and BOLE and
BLOSSOM and BONESHAKER and BUBONOCELE
and BEADBONNY and BINSEY and BURDEN and
BEREFT ...*

*Police and bailiffs gathered well before dawn to set the wheels
of Operation Barnard in motion. Commander John Townsend,
who was in overall charge of the operation, said: "This
operation is going to cause a lot of inconvenience to a lot of
people." Chief Superintendent Stuart Giblin predicted that local
residents would be joined by environmental campaigners from
across the country for the protest. He also feared that the
demonstration might be "hijacked" by militant left-wing groups.*

A Bailiff is an officer of the sherriff; a bumbailiff is an under-
bailiff. On 16 February 1994 the High Court Deputy Sherriff,
John Hargrove, who held three High Court writs for possession of numbers 4, 6 and 12 Cambridge Park, London E11,
and who was accompanied by 17 bailiffs and bumbailiffs, and
Brian Finch, Bow County Court Bailiff Manager, who held writs
for possession of numbers 2, 2A, 8 and 10 Cambridge Park,
London E11, and who was accompanied by 36 bailiffs and
bumbailiffs, served their warrants, ably assisted by some 600-
800 members of the Metropolitan Police, including members
of the Territorial Support Group wearing visors and helmets
and carrying tear gas.

SHERIFF. A county officer entrusted with the execution of
the laws. SHERIFF'S OFFICER: a bailiff. The Sheriff of Nott-
ingham. When William III returned from the Peace of Ryswick
he marched through London accompanied by sheriff's officers
with javelins, the aldermen, recorder and sheriffs all on horse-
back and in scarlet gowns ... 1887: The Sheriffs Act.

*Wiry heathpacks, flitches of fern,
And the beadbonny ash ...*

C

C is for CAPITALISM and CLARE and CHESTNUT and CHERRY-PICKER and CONSCIOUSNESS and CRITICISM and CYCLING ...

Anonymous. From *A Letter to Mr C–b–r On his Letter to Mr P—* (1742)

I can no more look upon coarse language to be true satire than I can rank gross lies under the head of poetic fiction . . . [Pope] has jumbled together my Lord Shaftesbury, Montaigne, Lora Herbert, Mandeville, and fifty et ceteras, till, from these fine uniform originals drawing only some incongruous scraps, his whole work is nothing but a heap of poetical contradictions, and a jarring series of doctrines, principles, opinions and sentiments, diametrically opposite to each other, making together just such an olio, hodge-podge mess of philosophy as one of Croe's best dinners would make of food.

*

Binsey Seven Twelve Ninety-Three. Shivering in the bitter December cold. T-shirt, shirt, woolen jumper, waxed jacket, still cold. "Here's to what was," as the man says in *The Blue Dahlia*. Went back two days later, old Johny Clare was there, yes there he was, not dead at all, a-gabbing away, like a loon, a loop, a-bellowing abuse at the security, at the hard-hats, at the putters-up of fences, the Green vanishing behind fenceposts. Made me think of Clare's poem, "Helpston Green", and in particular the lines:

> But now alas your awthorn bowers
> All desolate we see
> The tyrants hand their shade devours
> And cuts down every tree

In November 1993 Ellis Sharp copied these last two lines on to a placard constructed from the remains of breakfast cereal boxes and, after attending a protest at the tree one wet Saturday, fixed it in the damp earth, facing the traffic on the A12.

What sort of tree did you say it was?

A sweet chestnut *(Castanea sativa)*.

The sweet chestnut is a large, handsome tree with fine leaves and flowers, and distinctive twisting bark. The Romans spread it throughout Europe because the nuts were an important source of food to them. The first evidence of the presence of sweet chestnut in Britain is as charcoal fragments excavated from sites of Roman forts and villas. It does not readily establish itself in the wild and most of the specimens you see have been planted. Its normal span is about 500 years but many specimens exceed this. In old age the tree becomes grotesquely misshapen with a gigantic, gnarled trunk and huge twisted limbs. An enormous sweet chestnut grows in the grounds of Canford School, Dorset. The tree's bole is 13m (44 feet) in circumference – the greatest girth of any living tree in Britain.

My wits have gone on a fantastic ride ... Gerard Manley Hopkins tapping his foot to Terry Evans singing "I Want To Be Close To You, God". Hopkins checking out *The Golden Grove* pub in Stratford. Hopkins standing beside the traffic, shuddering ... Hopkins looking for the graves of the dead nuns in the cemetery. Listen, Hopkins may have been dead for a hundred years but I am claiming him for our side! He would have understood. The night, the blackness, the police. If on a winter's night a traveller had been passing, what might that traveller ... Me? Made me think of the Agony in the Garden, the armed men coming at night. Some of the protesters hugging the cops, kissing them, Christ how they hated it! Worried about the saliva of those fucking hippies! Terrified of catching AIDS! *Gerard? That's a poofter's name. You one of them fucking poofters, Hopkins?* George Green. George and the Dragon. Georgy Porgy Pudding & Pie. The girl with the split lip, punched in the face by a TSG cop. Whereas that arsehole

Tennyson *[believed to be a reference to Tennyson, Alfred, 1st Baron Tennyson. Ed.]* would have been on the other side, the dirty-long-haired-hippies-left-wing-agitators-send-'em-back-to-where-they-came-from brigade.

HIGH BEECH, Essex. Village off the A11 in Epping Forest. Tennyson lived at Beech House (rebuilt 1850) at the foot of Wellington Hill. Here he invested a legacy in a scheme to carve wood by machinery, established by the proprietor of the asylum, Fairmead (gone), where John Clare was sent in 1837. Tennyson probably remembered the inmates when writing *Maud* (1855). Edward Thomas was stationed here in the army in 1915 and a year later brought his family here to live in a cottage, where he spent his last Christmas with them before he was killed in France.

O chestnut-tree, great-rooted blossomer, Are you the leaf, the blossom or the bole?

And how precisely did the nineteenth-century Jesuit poet Gerard Manley Hopkins get to the site of the M11 link road in north-east London in January 1994? Like this. Mounting a woman's bicycle he pedalled briskly up the slight slope of Milton Road, London E17. And in what condition was this bicycle? Poor. Extensively pitted with rust. Stylish? Not in the least. Approximately thirty years old. Three gears. Wicker basket. A museum piece. And did Hopkins stop at the NO ENTRY sign at the junction with Byron Road? No, he did not. Listening carefully for the sound of internal combustion engines approaching from around the corner in Aubrey Road, he pedalled past the NO ENTRY sign, in flagrant defiance of road traffic regulations. And then? It depended on the day, the traffic, his mood. Sometimes he turned right and scooted down Aubrey Road, crossing Church Hill and pedalling along Folkestone Road, St Mary Road and East Avenue, then up Orford Road and along Beulah Road. Sometimes he did not turn right at Aubrey Road but left, scooting through the alley to Howard Road, then following Seaford Road to The Drive, crossing Church Hill and pedalling through the old churchyard, crossing Church End and, in flagrant defiance of the NO ENTRY

159

sign, along Orford Road until he reached Beulah Road. And then? Past the NO ENTRY sign and left down Maynard Road, cutting through to Barclay Road, sharp right along Shernhall Street, along Western Road, over the zebra crossing on Lea Bridge Road, along Peterborough Road, left at James Lane, right along Clare Road, left along Forest Road, right along Colworth Road, left up Preston Road, right along Poppleton Road, left up Ashbridge Road, right along Teesdale Road, across Leyton Way and along the pavement of Whipps Cross Road until he reached the pedestrian underpass at the Green Man roundabout, emerging on the far ramp and pedalling along the footway of Cambridge Park until just before the bus stop, where, in deference to pedestrians, he re-joined the carriageway. At this point the M11 link road site stretched ahead of him, into the distance, a series of long green fences topped with barbed wire and patrolled by yellow-jacketed security men wearing blue or white helmets.

More than 1,000 police and security guards moved in yesterday to end a protest by 300 squatters over a proposed £200 million motorway link road. Some of the hippy throng – many of whom spent the past 10 days barricaded into five derelict houses – were plucked from crumbling rooftops by bailiffs using two cranes.

*

LANGUAGE IS AS OLD AS CONSCIOUSNESS.
CONSCIOUSNESS IS, FROM THE VERY BEGINNING,
A SOCIAL PRODUCT.

D

D is for DICTIONARY and DONGA and DOWN and DREAM and DRINK ...

At the close of the seventeenth century Alexander Pope was

sent for a year's schooling at Twyford, a village three miles from Winchester. Above the village rose the green, curving slopes of Twyford Down, due to be vandalised forever some three hundred years later by an extension to the M3 motorway – a project involving a corrupt Government, a car- supremacist Department of Transport and the violence of "Yellow Wednesday", 9 December 1992, anticipating by almost exactly a year the events of "Blue Tuesday" in Wanstead, 7 December 1993.

*

COUNTDOWN TO THE END OF A DREAM

5.30 am – Police brief reporters and photographers about Operation Barnard.

7.00 am – Bailiffs shout warnings to the protesters over a tannoy system. The announcements were greeted by shouts, screams, drum beats, and sirens as protesters drowned out the bailiffs' warnings. The noise echoed around Wanstead.

7.30 am – In a tense and frightening atmosphere police moved in to clear the area and set up cordons. Onlookers described Wanstead as being part of a police state.

7.50 am – The first wall was pulled down by bailiffs. The haunting rhythms of the protesters' drums were rudely interrupted by smashes of the bailiffs' hammers.

8.00 am – Police with riot shields moved in as the first protesters were carried out of the cordon. Protesters in trees shouted support and encouragement to their colleagues.

8.25 am – Angus Richardson, one of the solicitors for the campaign, was removed from the house by police.

8.30 am – Chief Superintendent Stuart Giblin spoke to the media gathered on the other side of Cambridge Park.

8.40 am – First "cherry picker" moved into the area.

9.00 am – A number of people were removed from No. 10 Cambridge Park, including TV crews and reporters, who had spent the night with the protesters. One protester was dragged from a first floor window by three bailiffs. Fellow demonstrators alleged that he had been assaulted.

Solicitor Angus Richardson said: "For God's sake, watch that man's life!"

*

"Let's drink a toast."
"To Wanstonia."
"To Wanstonia!"

E

E is for ECO-WAR and EDITORIAL and EDMONTON and ELLIS and ELOISA and ENCYCLOPAEDISM and EPANAPHORA and EPISTLE and EXCESS ...

ROAD TO RUIN
Next time the police complain of undermanning, they must explain why they needed hundreds of men in riot gear to deal with a bunch of loops protesting against a new road.

(Editorial, *Today*, 17 February, 1994)

*

R—, scanning the crowd of protestors: "I can't see anyone from the Labour Party here today."

Ellis: "Well, there wouldn't be, would there? Just look at that fencing."

R— glanced at the four-metre-high security fencing coated with anti-climb paint and topped with three strands of barbed wire. "Ah, I see what you mean. Nowhere to sit."

*

AN EPISTLE TO JAMES ARBUTHNOT
See *Arbuthnot*, Wanstead's member i' the house,
His motions reminiscent of a louse,

162

See *Sporus* huff and wheedling leer
The anti-roads protesters are not from here.
A politician, said Cummings – and said it all,
For *Arbuthnot's* grossness is *not small*;
Arbuthnot's claims are false; are shit; a con:
Arbuthnot lives, vile Hypocrit, in Kensington.

*

Kevin Vaughan was a black anti-roads protester present in Wanstead on 16 February 1994. He was seized by five uni-formed police officers, who dragged him inside a white police Transit van. He was told he was being arrested for riotous assembly at Welling. He was taken to Edmonton police station for six hours while police searched through video film of the demonstration at Welling. He was told his face looked like the face of an alleged rioter published in the *Evening Standard*. But the photograph of the alleged rioter bore no resemblance to Kevin Vaughan. He was eventually released without charge.

(Paul Foot, "Prejudice that hands out rough justice",
The Guardian, 28 February 1994)

*

... we find [Pope] soon afterwards sprinkling his *Eloisa to Abelard* with epithets and phrases of a new form and sound, pilfered from *Comus* and the *Penseroso*.

(Thomas Warton, from the Preface to his edition of Milton's
Minor Poems [1785])

F

F is for FANCY

Why was not this simply expressed; without playing with the reader's fancy, to the delusion and dishonour of

his understanding ... the epitaphs of Pope cannot well
be too severely condemned; for not only are they almost
wholly destitute of those universal feelings and simple
movements of mind which we have called for as
indispensable, but they are little better than a tissue
of false thoughts, languid and vague expressions,
unmeaning antithesis, and laborious attempts at
discrimination.

(William Wordsworth, "Upon Epitaphs" [1810])

Chief Inspector Periphrasis, leaning against the squad car
door, using the sound system. "Under the Criminal Justice and
Public Order Act, 1994, I must warn you that the Creator of the
Universe has appointed every thing to a certain Use and
Purpose, and determined it to a settled Course and Sphere of
Action, from which, if it in the least deviates, it becomes unfit
to answer those Ends from which it was designed. I repeat:
ORDER is Heav'n's first law; and this confest, Some are, and
must be, greater than the rest, More rich, more wise. Therefore
in the name of Reason, Moderation, Decorum and Good Sense
I am ordering you all to disperse!"

"Yaaaaaaah! Wollawollawollawollawoooooooooh!"

G

G is for GIBLIN and GUIDE

*A short guide to the opposing forces involved in the
construction and obstruction of the M11 link road.*

capitalists	dongas
car supremacists	cyclists/pedestrians
roads	trees
phallic/male	polymorphous/androgynous/female
conformist	mutant

fundamentalist	dissident
fence	ladder
repression	liberation
work	play

*

The bailiffs deliberately began the demolition while the protesters were still in the building, and it is a miracle that no one was either struck by falling masonry or dropped from the "cherry-picker" hydraulic platforms. I watched with horror as sledgehammers and crowbars were used to smash up the roof around people's heads, while the protestors scrambled on loose slates and dangled dangerously over 30-foot drops. Back on the ground, I complained vigorously to the police commander of the operation, chief superintendent Stuart Giblin, who sneered that this was just what he would expect someone from the National Council for Civil Liberties to say.

(Conor Foley, *New Statesman* & *Society*, 25 February 1994)

H

H is for HAPPENING and HAVOC and HIPPY and HITS

When 55 bailiffs from Bow County Court arrived at 7 am, many of the protesters had painted their faces and were singing pagan chants and playing piccolos.

"What's happening?"

"Oh, *come on*! I would have thought that was *screamingly obvious*. What's happening is that the bulk of production and wealth in our society is being monopolised by a class which forms a tiny minority of the population and which is living off the profits extracted from the vast majority while at the same time controlling the state, i.e. the armed forces, the judiciary,

165

the police, the civil service etcetera etcetera while each posturing politician – a species so ably defined by the late great e. e. cummings – pretends that real power rests in Parliament rather than in board rooms and that political power is exercised in the interests of the people rather than the interests of the ruling class. In the case of the M11 Link Road we are faced with a classic example of this state of affairs. Beneath our very feet the Central Line of the London Underground system is crumbling away through neglect, with just weeks ago 20,000 people having to be led along the track after the 70-year-old electrical cabling failed, while £23 billion is being squandered on motorways by a corrupt and unpopular Government with a bankrupt transport policy!"

*

WHAT'S HAPPENING?
M-WAY DEMO HITS THE ROOF
STROKES OF HAVOC

I

I is for IDEOLOGIST ...

R.I.P. TREE
c. 1740-1993

... inside [the ruling] class one part appears as the thinkers of the class (its active, conceptive ideologists, who make the perfecting of the illusion of the class about itself their chief source of livelihood) ...

(Karl Marx and Frederick Engels, *The German Ideology*)

166

J

J is for **JOURNALISM ...**

BIG RON BLASTS HIS CUP FLOPS

SELF-STYLED REPUBLIC SMASHED BY POLICE

Beggar With L-Reg Astra Is Arrested

I'm Listening Says Major

COUNTDOWN TO THE END OF A DREAM

Queen Will Visit Russia To End Her 70-Year Feud

JAILBREAK COP-KILLER ON LOOSE

BURGER BLAST BOBBY TO SUE

MIKE KNOCKED OUT BY LITERATURE

SOS For Royal Yacht

TERROR OF TRAPPED TERRIER TOMMY

RISE IN JOBLESS AND INFLATION CHEERS CITY

THE BATTLE FOR WANSTONIA

Eco-Krakers Stoppen Snelweg

*

Putting aside mere idlers and sightseers and putting aside also a small band of persons with a diseased craving for notoriety the active portion of yesterday's mob was composed

167

of all that is weakest, most worthless, and most vicious of the slums of a great city. It was simple love of disorder, the revolt of dull brutality against the rule of law (*The Times,* 14 November, 1887).

Riot police skirmished with hundreds of protesters in east London yesterday as bulldozers demolished five Edwardian houses in the path of the M11 extension. Most of the demonstrators had arrived on coaches from all over Britain. Only a few came from Wanstead. The police included members of the Territorial Support Group in full riot gear. The officers went in at 7.30 am in wave after wave. The early morning silence, punctuated by the flutes and drums of the protesters, was shattered by the sound of breaking glass as the bailiffs, with sledgehammers and crowbars, crashed into the house (*The Times,* 17 February, 1994).

1. Spot the lie in the second extract. Candidates are allowed sixty seconds.

2. Discuss the role of Metropolitan Police Press Office press releases in reporting of major public order incidents in national daily newspapers. Candidates are allowed two hours.

3. Which British national newspaper did Karl Marx link with sewage, and why? One hour.

All questions are compulsory. All those failing to answer the first question correctly will automatically be suspended and only be permitted to return when they are able to display a close knowledge and understanding of Trotsky's *History of the Russian Revolution.*

K

K is for KEY and KISS and KNOTTY and

KNOWLEDGE and KRAKEN and KYMOGRAPH and
KYRIOLOGICAL ...

"What's happening?"

Good question, a very good question, a question which cannot be asked too often, especially where postmodernist fiction is concerned (say) or the crisis of contemporary capitalism (say) or of (be big, be bold) reality, that even greyer, worn-down noun, smooth as a Chesil pebble, lodged in Violet Cullingford's old dictionary – *To Violet with best wishes from Bill and Evelyn 13/3/1933* – on the same page as READORN and READVERTENCY and READY-WITTED and REAFFOREST and REAPPORTION and REARISE and REARMAMENT and REARRANGEMENT (not to mention the last monitory published by the Romish Church after three admonitions and before the last excommunication or the reremouse or a royal jurisdiction or a bundle of paper consisting of twenty quires or the lowest grade of commodore), the location of which chiefly appealed to Hopkins not because of these jostling, squeaking companions but because REALITY lay south-west of REAPING-HOOK, the only word to be blessed with an illustration, about an inch high, calling to mind the defunct Union of Soviet Socialist Republics and strongly resembling a question mark.

Greyer than *what*? a whisper went.

Greyer even than the cold grey eye of the TV news team's camera pointing down at him from between the barbed wire – or was it not (change angle of vision, adjust the lighting) black? A black hole sucking for good footage, pics 'n' words suitable for fashioning into that commodity called NEWS, tidings, new or interesting information, fresh events, which a moment's carelessness can turn into a small-tailed amphibian.

L

L is for LAND and LANGUAGE and LEAR and
LEYTONSTONIA and LOOPS and LOST and LOVE

and LOWRY and LONDON TONIGHT …

That time in the desert. Lost. The cold wind in your face. Tired and stiff, you walked and walked and walked. Dog-tired, in the cold and rain, you lay down to sleep. When you woke you found it difficult to remember where you were or what you were doing. So perishingly cold. Clothes soaked and the cold wind in your face. *What's happening? What's happening? What's happening?* All you had to eat was a bar of chocolate, which you ate. A mouthful of water. Then on, walking, walking, walking. Numbed, mind emptied out. Sat down, fell asleep, woken by the bitter cold. The day wearing out, perishing amid a perishing cold. And then the sudden solitary flute, the far-off trilling. Silvery Mozart. Silenced as soon as started. You walked on, half-hearing the kettle-drum, gone. Later, a violin, infinitely mournful, something by Mahler. Fades out. The low whine of the wind gusting across desolate grey sand. More kettle-drum, then fades. Grey and cold, the rain, a soft pattering. Rain stops. So perishingly cold. Walking, walking, walking. Clothes soaked, shivering. An entire orchestra flooding suddenly your mind, a tremendous cacophonous reverberant demented tumult, Shostakovich's Eleventh, at full blast, flicked into nothing by the sound of an engine, a blue VW coming up the track behind you. A green-eyed woman with her hair done up in a bun like Queen Victoria on an old penny; Martina. Her radio playing "Sweet Baby James".

*

On Tuesday 26 January 1994 the land at 187/189 Fillebrook Road, London E11, was occupied by squatters as the first piece of land forming part of Leytonstonia, one of the three independent free areas belonging to the confederation recently initiated in Wanstonia. Legal "squatter" notices on the corrugated iron boundary fences were correctly placed but despite this demolition contractors entered the site with the intention of chainsawing trees. Police and campaign lawyer

Angus Richardson were called to the site. On arrival, Richardson explained the law to the police inspector in charge as it applied to squatters and their rights and was laughed at by the inspector. A representative of the Department of Transport then telephoned the DoT solicitors to obtain instructions, and the contractors and police then withdrew. "The law on this land is the same as that for the ancient chestnut-tree house on George Green near Wanstonia," said Richardson. "All we can do in effect is to force the DoT to act within the law." An Order 113 is likely to be applied for and granted. Later the same day a man was seen trying to enter the site by removing a panel of corrugated iron. When challenged he walked off. A few minutes later he returned and when approached by an occupier of the land, he hurled a half-brick hitting the victim on the forehead above the eye, knocking him unconscious.

*

... something along the lines of Malcolm Lowry's "Through the Panama" (a title which surely echoes Lewis Carroll's *Through the Looking Glass*). Though "Through the Panama" doesn't entirely lack linearity and chronology it's more a vast, encyclopaedic collage of fragments drawing together – or at any rate, juxtaposing – the private and public worlds of the writer and his obsessions ... "To Wanstonia" also sets out to make a perverse connection between Alexander Pope, Twyford Down and the No M11 Link Road campaign. What's more – [here another section of the manuscript is missing].

*

Six arrests ... "Two of those arrested, we understand, were detained at the Welling riot last year, which might give you some idea of outside interests involved in this operation."
(Christopher Peacock, Carlton TV news reporter, speaking live from the ruins of Wanstonia on the 6 p.m. *London Tonight* news programme, 16 February 1994.)

M

M is for MARXISM and MEANWHILE and METAFICTION and MISCELLANEOUS and METROPOLITAN POLICE COMMISSIONER ...

The Sergeant scowled at Hopkins. "Jesuit fucking experimental poet? Don't make me bloody laugh. I've had enough of you bloody literary types coming up here causing trouble. Christ, only last week we had a metafictionist in here. Shooter or Shorts or Shaper or somesuch. Well, the moment I saw him I knew he was trouble. *Open that bag*, I said. Just as I expected. Peanut butter sandwiches, a camera and a slimline edition of *Socialism: Utopian and Scientific*. I told him straight. *I've met your sort before*, I said. *I know your tricks. Effacing your subjectivities behind surrogates. Keeping people awake at night with a plurality of selves. Well, let me tell you something*, I said. *I've had it up to here with you fucking ontological amphibians,* I said. You just watch it my lad, I said. Epigrammatic tendencies *ain't natural.* Bloody literary pervert, I thought. Composing filthy foreign *feuilletons. Accreting paragraphs* with no respect for linearity. Practising condensation with the curtains drawn. It's offensive. Me, I'm an R. F. Delderfield man, my wife prefers Lena Kennedy. You meet a lot of different people in my job and if there's one thing I know it's this. *We don't want metafiction in Wanstead.* We're not that sort of people. P. D. James is quite good enough for the likes of us, mister hoity-toity experimentalist. You just get back to bloody Hampstead or Hackney or wherever you sodding crawled from. Don't let me catch you this side of the Green Man roundabout again or else I'll charge you with *hontological vacillation*. And I'll tell you something else. The magistrates is very tough on that up here. You can count on four weeks inside at least. And I'm saying the same thing to you. Hoppit, Hopkins. Git. Scarper. Get thee gone."

Hopkins moved towards the door, but the sergeant, remembering the conventions of soap opera, called out to him, causing him to turn, permitting a further sixty-five seconds of dialogue.

"And another thing."

Hopkins looking back; Hopkins keenly alert to what is about to be said, for he has always been interested in the things that follow things, transience, the bereavements and howling griefs positioned inconspicuously amongst the sand-supported amoeba-restless shadows of those healthy, sunlit ball-tossing bodies on summer's brilliant beach, patient as Stonehenge, biding their time, waiting to pounce in the name of all that perishes, skin and hair and teeth and bone and stone and brick and wood and rubber and ink, friendships and marriages, the sphinx and the writing on Shakespeare's will, the willows and the hawthorn trees on Helpston Green, Binsey Poplars, the trees at the edge of Cambridge Park, the wind and the rain, the bulldozer's loud grind and drone and the barely audible death-rattle at the edge of all that party laughter, sweet necessary dread transience delivering with conveyor-belt regularity one thing after another, always, always another thing, the rust after the rain, Stalin after Lenin, grey morning after fiery night, soft paper tissues after sex, sleep after toyle, port after stormie seas.

The Sergeant fell silent; looked confused.

"And?" *Come along man! I am Gerard Manley Hopkins, an important nineteenth-century poet. I haven't got all day.*

"That chap Scarp. It wasn't true I let him go. I charged him under Section 52 of the Criminal Justice and Public Order Act 1994 with having committed aestho-autogamy. And you know what happened? He at once pulled out a pair of nail scissors and started paring his fingernails. Disgusting. Of course I told him to put them away, but a funny thing happened. My voice just seemed to go. I couldn't speak a word. Next there was a sort of white flash, and I can hear this Shark bloke saying something about he's tired and it's time for bed. Then – CLICK! Everything vanishes and starts to go cold. I'm completely in the dark about what's happening. I can't seem to move any of my limbs. Talk about Repetitive Strain Injury! It's

173

like I'm totally paralysed. I start to remember a horrible article I once read in the *Daily Telegraph* magazine about a man who went off to catch a train at Waterloo Station and suddenly went blind. I can hear footsteps padding about, the clatter of washing-up, Leonard Cohen and Elton John singing "Born to Lose". Next day I'm woken by a strange humming noise, like a hard disk starting up. I found myself lying in a snow covered field. White everywhere. And incredibly cold. To cut a long story short, somehow I managed to make it over the page and back to Wanstead. I'll never know how I did it. And I'll tell you something else. It makes me sick to hear people going on and on and on about Henry James's father being struck down near Windsor Park by a sense of nothingness which overwhelmed him in spite of its being an agreeable summer evening, all pinkish blue sky and far-off birds flopping homeward to cosy nests and his digestive system dealing magnificently with mouthful upon mouthful of breaded scampi and chipped potatoes, a moment of horror he could not get over for weeks, for months, for years, a horror that haunted him even unto death, making him sweat and tremble and feel ill-at-ease, even on the pleasantest of days, his wife beaming like a banana, a child blowing soap bubbles, a nearby drunken brass band merrily attempting Schoenberg's Wind Quintet Op. 26. *Henry James's father should have gone through what I had to go through*. Finding your way through the tangle of a post-modernist story is no joke. You lot think you've got problems getting over those fences and through all that barbed wire and on to the M11 Link Road site. You should think about how it is for *me*. Ever since we arrested Spook I've suffered from headaches, migraine, rheumatic and muscular pains, defective vision, backache, pains and feverishness requiring constant decoctions of acacia bark, poppy heads, quince seeds, compound sarsaparilla and Irish moss."

Hopkins smiled wanly, nodded thoughtfully, grinned wistfully, shrugged, jitterbugged, shook his head, at first mysteriously and then whimsically. "Painted or not painted, all shall fade," he whispered. Pausing only to autograph the

Sergeant's paperback copy of *Poems of Gerard Manley Hopkins*, he departed.

Once outside in the High Road he set off at a brisk pace in search of a bus stop.

*

Tennyson said: "I regret to say the disruption in the forest is as bad as ever. The M11 Link Road protesters have managed to recruit John Clare and Gerard Manley Hopkins for their cause, and there are rumours William Morris has been seen on Wanstead flats selling *Socialist Worker*. The Chief Superintendent has privately informed me that he believes militant postmodernists are masterminding the protests."

*

E.R.

Monday, 21 March 1994

Written No. 168
(16.3.94)

Mr Neil Gerrard (Walthamstow): To ask the Secretary of State for the Home Department, how many people were arrested during Operation Barnard in Wanstead on 16 February on suspicion of having been involved in a riot at Welling last October; and of these how many were subsequently released without any charges being brought.

MR CHARLES WARDLE

I understand from the Metropolitan Police Commissioner that five people were arrested on suspicion of having been involved in disturbances at Welling. All were subsequently released without charge.

\

N is for NARRATIVE and NASEBY and NIETZSCHE and NONSENSE ...

The moustache seemed a long time ago, now, Bodrum thought.

*

A STRANGE WILD LINSEY-WOLSEY COMPOSITION, AN IDLE EMPTY TRIFLING PIECE OF NONSENSE, THE WHOLE PIECE SO NOTORIOUSLY FULL OF PRIDE, INSOLENCE, BEASTLINESS, MALICE, PROFANENESS, CONCEITS, ABSURDITIES, AND EXTRAVAGANCE THAT 'TIS ALMOST IMPOSSIBLE TO FORM A REGULAR NOTION OF IT

*

sleepy doll's adventure

One day sleepy doll went to the forest. She saw a snake. "What is your name?" said sleepy doll. "Tom" he said then sleepy doll saw a dog. Sleepy said SSS. He ran to the snake. "There's a snake." While they were chatting sleepy doll locked them in a cage. She laughed. "Heh heh heh" went sleepy doll.

*

The Descriptions are singular; the Comparisons very quaint; the Narration various, yet of one colour. As it beareth the name of Epic, it is thereby subjected to a strict imitation of the antient. How exact that Imitation hath been in this piece appeareth not only by its general structure, but by particular allusions infinite, many whereof have escaped both the commentator and the poet himself; yea divers by his exceeding diligence are so alter'd and interwoven with the rest, that several have already been, and more will be, by the ignorant abused, as altogether and originally his own.

This is the story of Mr Triangle

One sunny day there was a girl called Louise. She went to the park to play. There was a bush in the park. She liked to play near it with her friend. Her friend was called Natasha. Natasha and Louise were playing skipping by the bush. Suddenly the bush moved! and out of the bush came a triangle. "Hello what is your name?" said Louise. "I don't have a name," said the triangle. "Then we will give you a name," said Natasha. "What will you call me?" said the triangle. "Mr Triangle," said Natasha.

The End.

The M11 link road

Once upon a time there was a capitalist society with a bourgeois parliamentary democracy where the transport system was in chaos because it operated according to the anarchic laws of the capitalist market and where the ruling political party had long been financed by road hauliers and manufacturers of roadbuilding materials who hated public transport, railways, buses, cyclists and pedestrians. By 1994 the Government was squandering £23 billion on an extravagant and irrational roads programme, while public transport decayed and healthy forms of mobility such as walking and cycling were marginalised, discriminated against and made dangerous and unpleasant. On Tuesday 14th September 1993 work began on the M11 link road in Wanstead, north-east London. It was a road which was intended to link the end of the M11 motorway with the A102(M) in Hackney, a Borough where 61.7% of households did not possess a car. The work began with the destruction of three acres of trees in Wanstead and, over the next four years, required the demolition of some 300 homes. Opposition to the link road now began to involve "direct action" and developed a narrative momentum of its own. In September 1993 derelict houses in Wanstead were occupied and sections of the roadbuilding site were regularly invaded by small groups of protesters, seeking to save trees and hold up work by lying in front of bulldozers; in October attention focused on George Green, Wanstead, where a sweet chestnut tree estimated to be some 250-275 years old was due to be bulldozed. Protesters occupied the tree and built a tree house in its branches. When the roadbuilders fenced off the tree and tried to starve out the tree-squatters a crowd gathered and tore down the fencing. The tree became famous and four hundred letters from well-wishers were delivered by the local postman. A High Court judge determined that the tree was a lawful dwelling, a judgement quickly quashed. In the early hours of 2 December, ere Phoebus rose, a petrol bomb attack was made both on the tree and on an adjacent tent where campaigners were sleeping; two men from Southend were caught by the campaigners and subsequently charged with arson with intent to endanger life. Our narrative now comes to the extraordinary events of 7 December 1993.

It was a moonless, bitterly cold night. The rain pelted down in brief bursts, then ebbed to a light shower. Even though Ellis Sharp was wearing a T-shirt under a thick cotton shirt, and a woolen jumper under a substantial waxed country jacket, he shivered and trembled with cold. Arriving at George Green at 4.35am he saw that there was not only a crowd around the chestnut tree, but that there were also protesters in the trees at the corner of Draycot Road and Cambridge Park. The strange wailing-bleating of a bullhorn erupted loudly from dark branches high above him, cutting through the rustling, rainy night. A lantern glowed high in the tree, a soft purple-blue against a harsh, racing, wintry sky. Sharp hurried on to join the crowd around the tree, expecting forty or fifty, astonished at the numbers who'd turned out, a good two hundred, maybe more, impossible to tell accurately, dense circles of protesters ringing the old swollen trunk, features steeped in the muddy orange of soggy sodium from the nearest streetlights, dark shapes moving slowly in the wind-shaken foliage above. And then the tempest struck.

For twenty minutes it raged, pounding us all, a force 7 Westerly rising 8, roaring up Cambridge Park, squall upon squall.

And then, shortly before 5.30 am, flashing blue lights of police motorcycle outriders appeared, approaching from Eastern Avenue. Closer they came, escorting a cavalcade of fifteen police Transit vans, three khaki-green police coaches and a fleet of ambulances. Here were the sheriff's officers, accompanied by 371 police officers, arriving under cover of darkness to evict protesters and allow the tree to be bulldozed.

At once the alarm call of the Dongas tribe rang out, "ARR-OOGA! ARROOGA!" – *our land is threatened*!

O

O *is for **OBSCURITY** and **OBSTIPATION** and **OBSTRUCTION** and **OCTOGENARIAN** and **ODD** and **OLIO** ...*

OLIO, *n.* oh-le-o, a mixture; a medley; a miscellaneous stew. (Sp.)

Without warning, the police rushed at the people around the tree and began to pull them away, dragging at clothes, hair, ears, eyes, noses, genitals. *There was screaming from those in pain, as well as those trying to protect each other and reason with the police, some of whom were striking out indiscriminately.* Four people formed an inner defensive ring, locking their hands together inside heavy steel tubes around the trunk of the tree. The police formed a large circle around the tree, each officer holding the waistband of the trousers worn by the officer in front. *It appeared that they were not, as we had enquired, preparing to do the 'okey-cokey, but were waiting for a hydraulic platform (known as a "cherry-picker") to tackle the six men and one woman who had secured themselves in a number of ingenious ways to the upper branches.*

P

P is for PANIC and PAGAN and PARANOIA and PERFORMANCE and PERIPHRASIS and PHOEBUS and PIG and PICCOLOS and PLANT and POLICE and POPE and PRIEST and POSTMODERNISM and PROTESTER and PSYCHIATRIST ...

At a meeting of the Redbridge Police-Community Consultative Group held at Redbridge Technical College near Romford on 18 January 1994 Chief Superintendent Stuart Giblin of Ilford Police said that where protests against the M11 link road were concerned the police were "pig in the middle".

*

"Of course not many people realise that the government's £23 billion roads programme is in reality a plot to erase all physical traces of this country's socialist and revolutionary history! The battlefield of Naseby, for example!" "I know what you mean. All those times I've marched down Whitehall and I've never been too clear where they cut off Charles I's head." "Not to mention the heads of the Duke of Hamilton, the Earl of Holland and Lord Capel." "In the case of the M11 Link Road there can be little doubt this is a massive cover-up to eliminate the spot on Leyton High Road where Cornelius Cardew was assassinated by the security service!"

*

DIVISION OF LABOUR ONLY BECOMES TRULY
SUCH FROM THE MOMENT WHEN A DIVISION OF

MATERIAL AND MENTAL LABOUR APPEARS. (THE
FIRST FORM OF IDEOLOGISTS, *PRIESTS,* IS
CONCURRENT.)

*

... A PERFORMANCE CONSISTING, AS IT SEEMS,
OF MANY FRAGMENTS WROUGHT INTO ONE DESIGN
(Samuel Johnson on Pope's "Epistle to Dr. Arbuthnot")

*

*In 1734 the poet Alexander Pope stayed at Bolingbroke's Farm
and from there went on to stay at Rousham and from there to
stay with Lord Cobham and from there travelling on to
Cirencester and also calling in at Amesbury, Twickenham
and Tottenham, from where he made his only visit to the
village of Wanstead in Essex, planting a sweet chestnut on
common land east of the track leading down towards Leyton
Stone ...*

*

"The avalanche," said Maisie fiercely. "That's what."

"Avalanche?" said Bodrum, frowning. "What avalanche?"
Did she mean the song "Avalanche" by Leonard Cohen, of
which he knew three versions, the one he liked least (Cohen's),
and the two he particularly liked (Nick Cave's and Jean-Louis
Murat's)?

No, she didn't.

I mean *this,* she said fiercely, handing him a paperback with
a stark green and white cover. *To Wanstonia.* By Ellis Sharp.
The name seemed dimly familiar. Once, long ago, tangled up in
Nietzsche ...

Mist. Confusion. Dense thickets.

She opened it, found the last page, pointed with her finger.
"There. See?"

Bodrum nodded absently. His mind lay elsewhere. "Is the book any good?"

"How should I know? It's 9.54 pm on Monday January 31st 1994 and the book isn't written yet. Ask me again in a year's time."

"What's Sharp doing now?"

"He's about to press QUIT, by the look of it. I expect he wants to watch a bit more of *Lady Macbeth of Mtsensk,* then switch over to catch the local news to see if there's anything on about Wanstonia."

"Wanstonia?"

"Half a dozen large derelict Edwardian properties at Cambridge Park, Wanstead. They're all that's left in the way of building an important section of the M11 Link Road in Wanstead, east London. The campaigners against the road have dubbed the houses "Wanstonia" as a publicity-stunt and all the houses have been occupied. A judge refused to allow the eviction of the protesters because the Department of Transport hadn't followed the correct procedures but the case went back to the High Court today and the eviction will probably get the green light."

"Run for it, Maisie!
    He's
        about
            to
                press –"

O Revolution! Thou dost not await the well-timed day and hour. Thou comest suddenly, blind and fatal as the avalanche.

Prosper-Olivier Hipployte Lissagaray (1876)

www.ingramcontent.com/pod-product-compliance
Lightning Source LLC
Chambersburg PA
CBHW032204190626
46810CB00018B/1396